Savage Rides West

Railroad baron Lew Preston fears his daughter Barbara might be kidnapped on her journey to marry his associate Jerry Crowther. So Savage, Pinkerton's toughest agent, is hired to escort her by rail from Chicago to California.

The demure red-headed Barbara is soon revealed as a hellion. 'Red' shows she can rough it when the train is wrecked, and she and Savage join a wagon travelling west. Then, a gang of crooks grab Red, and Savage risks his life in rescuing her. He realizes that Red is a reluctant bride, but doggedly continues west with the girl in tow. But on reaching Crowther in San Francisco, they are caught up in a maelstrom of treachery and torture.

Has Savage completed his assignment only to find death?

Savage Rides West

Sydney J. Bounds

A Black Horse Western

ROBERT HALE · LONDON

ISBN 978-0-7090-8347-4

Robert Hale Limited
Clerkenwell House
Clerkenwell Green
London EC1R 0HT

Typeset by
Derek Doyle & Associates, Shaw Heath
Printed and bound in Great Britain by
Antony Rowe Limited, Wiltshire

CHAPTER 1

'Go West, Young Woman!'

The railroad depot was crowded and noisy. It seemed almost alive, seething with travellers and visitors, porters, confidence men and police. It echoed with a babble of voices, the hissing of steam and drip of water, excited shouts and curses. The departure of the transcontinental express was still enough of a novelty to attract sightseers.

Savage stood a little way off from his party, watchful, under the clocks and close to a news stand. Some people looked up at the clocks to see the time in each zone across the continent: other people grabbed a paper or magazine for the journey. Either way, they helped to screen him with their quick darting movements.

He stood quietly, carrying his shotgun, a big Bowie knife sheathed beneath his suit coat. He was not tall and a wide-brimmed Stetson shadowed what had once been called a 'babyface' but now showed lines of experience. He wore a string tie with a white shirt and high heeled boots: his gear was already aboard.

The hat was because he knew that once beyond the hills and trees and onto the open plain the sun would boil the brains of any greenhorn.

His attention centred on a neatly dressed young woman with flame-red hair; Barbara Preston, daughter of Lew Preston, the railroad baron. She was the target and his to protect.

Lew, who was paying Pinkerton's for his services, looked old enough to be her grandfather. His suit hung loosely, his face was creased by worry and his grey hair almost white.

Nell, Barbara's maid, looked hardly older than her mistress, and bubbled with excitement. Her figure was well-padded and she had the lilt of the Irish in her voice. Just now she was being important and overseeing the luggage being portered to the baggage van. There was not as much as Savage had feared and that Barbara Preston travelled light surprised him. The two women made him think of an actress and her dresser.

His glance passed on, over the crowd, and

paused at a young man hovering behind the Prestons. Any man might take an interest in a young and attractive woman; he imagined she collected admirers the way others collected butterflies or postage stamps. So was this one taking more than a passing fancy?

He was young, his suit cleaned and pressed – possibly a clerk – and an impressionable female might consider him handsome if she ignored his pale city skin. His most obvious feature was a pair of smart new boots.

A loud voice brayed through the jungle of sounds: 'All aboard! This train is about to leave for the west coast, calling at Omaha, Cheyenne, Salt Lake and all points between!'

Nell and the luggage had already disappeared aboard, and Savage lost sight of the young man as passengers surged forward, climbing the steps to the cars.

Preston briefly embraced his daughter, then stepped back. 'Be good, Barbara.'

'Of course, Dad!' Did she wink?

Savage followed, lingering by the carriage door, looking out. Had the young man boarded? Lew Preston didn't wait to wave as the train moved out, but turned abruptly and hurried away. Savage frowned, feeling he was missing something.

He located Barbara's compartment – she was

sharing with Nell – and checked it out. Was she really at risk? he wondered. She didn't act scared. He decided to have a word with the conductor later.

There was a jolting motion; then the depot began to slide away as the train picked up speed.

Savage claimed a seat where he could watch the door of Barbara's compartment. The car swayed. Wheels *clackety-clacked* over joins in the rails: the city faded behind them as the train headed west for the open prairie.

Savage was amused. This office, in Pinkerton's Chicago agency, was startlingly different from Mr Allan's in New York. The room where he had first been interviewed was a working office, lined with files, musty-smelling, and his chair hard wood with a straight back.

This office, once past the brass plate reading *W.A. Pinkerton,* was larger with well-upholstered chairs, leatherbound books in a glass-fronted case and a selection of coloured maps on the walls.

It was, he thought, an office designed to impress clients; and so these two waiting for him must be important enough to bring him here from the south-west division on Mr Allan's recommendation. He saw a middle-aged man and a young woman.

Savage removed his hat and her gaze went immediately to the white streak in his hair.

8

Mr William stood to introduce them, and Savage noted the family likeness to Allan Pinkerton, despite the heavy beard that hid most of his face.

'Lew Preston, one of this country's finest railroad builders and his daughter, Barbara.'

Preston was still a man to be reckoned with. Savage got the impression he had been a large man who'd shrunk and now his clothes appeared too big for him.

The young woman, a redhead had blue eyes, a gaze that pierced and, Savage detected, a full figure confined by a high-necked dress.

'Mr Savage, one of our most experienced detectives and specifically recommended by Mr Allan will be handling your problem. Incidentally he knows San Francisco from a previous assignment.'

Barbara Preston gave him a speculative look, as if assessing the phrase 'most experienced'.

Lew Preston said, 'Barbara is taking the train, with her maid, to California. She is marrying Jerry Crowther, my opposite number out there. He runs the Pacific end of the railroad network we're developing to criss-cross this fine country of ours. A lifetime's work, I might add.'

He jabbed a finger. 'Your job, Mr Savage, is to make sure she reaches Crowther. While you may consider this as simple escort duty, keep in mind that a man in my position makes enemies. They may try to kidnap Barbara to strike at me through her. No doubt you'll know what I mean.'

Savage nodded, running a fresh eye over his assignment. She had the surface appearance of a demure, well brought up young lady: but her red hair could prove a danger signal.

'Enemies?' he echoed. 'Can you name them? Who do I look out for. Give me a description.'

'Could be anyone,' Preston said hurriedly. 'Anyone at all. Moneyed people tend to stay in the background and hire others to do their dirty work.'

Savage looked hard at the railroad baron and wondered: was he being deliberately vague?

Beyond the river, the train rattled along at speed. The long journey was well under way, passengers relaxed and taking an interest in what lay outside the windows. Every window in every direction: flat grassland baked brown by the sun.

Savage relaxed too, hat tilted forward to shade his eyes. Heat was beginning to build and, here and now, it seemed unlikely anyone would try to snatch the Preston girl. He dozed.

'We're going to eat.'

Barbara's voice came sharp and unfriendly. He opened his eyes, instantly alert. 'I'll join you.'

'I thought you might.'

They walked along the swaying corridor, with

her maid following, to the dining car and sat together at one table. Barbara got immediate attention and they ordered.

Savage said, 'Your father was vague on the subject of enemies. Have you noticed anyone suspicious hanging around?'

Barbara shrugged and didn't bother to answer, and he turned to Nell. 'Have you seen anyone taking an unusual interest?'

The Irish maid rolled her eyes. 'I wish. No one ever seems to notice me.'

Their meals arrived and shortly after the young man with new boots Savage had noted at the depot.

'Not again,' Barbara said. 'Go away. Mr Savage, make him leave me alone.'

The young man grinned. 'I'm not going anywhere, not till you agree to marry me.'

Savage came to his feet. 'You heard the lady, so take a walk.'

'Think you can make me?'

A Bowie knife appeared in Savage's hand, its point touching the young man's throat: as it drew a bead of blood he took a step back.

'You've no right to threaten me!'

A black conductor hurried towards them. 'No trouble please, gents,'

'No trouble,' Savage agreed. 'Perhaps you'll escort this young man back to his seat. He's bothering the lady.'

'I wasn't bothering her at all,' the young man said indignantly. 'My name's Frank Abbey and she knows me and I'm asking her to marry me. She's not married yet, you know.'

'Why don't you check his ticket,' Savage suggested.

Abbey reached into a pocket and showed the paste-board: Savage made a mental note of which pocket.

'Just stay away from Miss Preston,' Savage repeated.

The conductor turned to Barbara. 'Is this fellar really annoying you, Miss?'

She smiled and remained silent. Nell murmured, 'He's sweet on her is all.'

Abbey laughed and walked away with the conductor. 'I'll see you again, Barbara. You'll change your mind yet.'

Savage heard him talking to the conductor. 'It's not true an army marches on its stomach. We won the war because we had the best boots. . . .'

Savage sheathed his knife and sat down to finish his meal.

Savage stretched like a cat as the conductor walked the length of the coach, calling: 'Omaha next stop. If you want to exercise your legs, you have fifteen minutes.'

As the train began to slow, Frank Abbey appeared again. 'Fancy a walk with me, Barbara?'

'Go away!'

'I'm going,' the young man said, and Savage followed him along the corridor.

The train swayed to a stop and Savage crowded Abbey as he opened the door to step down to the platform. The young man elbowed him back. 'Get off me!'

'Sorry,' Savage said lightly, and moved away. He saw Abbey walk along to the window of Barbara's compartment and tap on it. She ignored him.

Savage strolled up and down. The young man began to distribute leaflets to people on the platform. Savage rescued one that was immediately discarded and shoved it in his pocket.

He watched as a water hose swung over the locomotive's boiler to fill it, and coal tumbled down a chute into the tender.

A station porter shouted, 'All aboard!' Savage tapped him on the shoulder, showed his credentials and spoke quietly. The porter looked towards Abbey, and nodded.

Savage was last aboard and slammed the door after him. He smiled as he saw Abbey searching his pockets. The locomotive's whistle shrilled out, the wheels turned and the train began to roll forward.

The porter had Abbey's arm in a firm grip as he

tried to board, until the last coach passed by at increasing speed.

Now Savage ran an eye over the leaflet he'd rescued:

ABBEY *and* SON
of Chicago for:
Quality Boots
All leather, built by craftsmen
for riding, walking, working
hard wearing and competitively priced.
Ladies shoes to order.
Abbey Boots are good for your feet!

Smiling, Savage returned to his seat and found Barbara waiting. 'What happened to Frank?'

'It seems he lost his ticket.'

She regarded him with admiration. 'I like that – it's kind of neat.'

The hours passed as the train crossed an endless prairie, but it seemed that no sooner had he got rid of one admirer than another popped up: this time, one of Nell's.

Savage viewed him with suspicion, but it could be true. Nell, though solidly built, was not unattractive. Their talk sounded serious and Nell looked happy.

This one was older, with a sharp gaze and a

pointed nose and called himself 'Dave'. Savage talked to Barbara, who shrugged.

'He's told Nell he's a journalist, writing a book about the overland journey. Even an Irish maid is entitled to a love life, Mr Savage. Off duty, of course.'

'Could be he aims to reach you through her.'

'I don't think so.'

'You could arrive in San Francisco without a maid.'

'So I'll hire another.' Barbara Preston abruptly changed her tone. 'You can make yourself useful – fetch my trunk from the baggage van.'

Savage stared. 'That's not my job.'

Her eyes sparked. 'I'm paying you, so you'll do what I tell you!'

He shook his head. 'It's your father who's paying Pinkerton's. And my job is to deliver you to Mr Crowther.'

'Crowther!' For a moment he thought she was going to spit. Her nostrils flared.

Nell knew the danger signs and disappeared in a hurry.

A redhead with a temper, Savage thought: Jerry Crowther could be getting more than he bargained for.

He returned to his seat and closed his eyes. A little later he heard two females, heads close together, giggling.

CHAPTER 2

A CHANGE OF WHEELS

The train hurtled along at what Savage assumed to be its best speed. The coach rocked and swayed. Beyond the curtained windows – curtained to keep out the glare of the sun – the prairie stretched like an endless ocean of brown grass.

Only once had there been a change of scenery, when they slowed to use a trestle bridge and, below, saw the dried-up bed of a river with a bare trickle of water in its centre. As the heat built up, tempers shortened.

Even Nell snapped at her journalist admirer. 'Not now, it's too hot.'

Outside a heat haze lay over the treeless plain;

inside few people were wide awake. The hypnotic *clackety-clack* of wheels was suddenly drowned out by thunder: but this thunder didn't come from the sky. Something vast and heaving rippled across the land. People jerked back curtains to stare in wonder.

'An earthquake,' someone said.

'Buffalo,' an old hand corrected. 'Must be one of the last herds.'

Then came a scattering of Indians, on horseback, hunting them. For several minutes passengers were held spell-bound, thrilling to the skill and excitement of the chase.

The herd appeared as a dense brown carpet composed of hairy humps surging across the land, a living mass that was almost beyond belief.

Then, without warning, the leaders changed direction and started to cross the railroad track in front of the train. Once the leaders were across, the rest of the herd followed.

Savage heard a shriek of steam and a squeal of metal as the engineer applied the brakes in an attempt to stop the train. He was too late. The locomotive, weighing several tons, had barely begun to slow when it ploughed into a heaving mass of flesh and bone.

The coach shuddered and swayed wildly. The wheels lost traction and slipped and the whole train began to tilt.

'Down,' Savage snapped. 'Get down!' The two women followed his lead.

Metal strained and woodwork snapped, glass shattered. The noise escalated, wounded animals bellowing, injured passengers screaming or sobbing.

A rumble of hoofs faded as the living buffalo and Indians swept on into the distance as if it had all been a dream. For a moment, a great silence descended.

Savage picked himself up and pulled Barbara to her feet.

She appeared calm, he noted with approval, and pushed her out of the coach. Other passengers joined her beside the derailed train.

He took a quick look at Nell, one leg twisted under her, and her face white. 'Can you walk if I get you upright?'

The maid looked past him. Barbara's head showed where the window had been, and she murmured, 'Dave's coming.'

Nell sagged back against what had been the floor, closed her eyes and sighed. Savage heard footfalls behind him and turned quickly, but it was only Nell's journalist.

'You'll take care of her, won't you, Dave?' Barbara said. 'She seems really shaken.'

'You bet, ma'am. It's my intention to do that on a permanent basis.'

Barbara closed one eye and withdrew. Savage followed her outside. He collected his gear and left it with her. 'Stay in the shade,' he told her and went forward.

There were dead bodies in the first coach and he helped himself to their canteens. The locomotive's boiler was leaking and he filled each one, taking care not to be scalded by steam. It was obvious the train wasn't going anywhere until a repair crew arrived.

He rejoined Barbara. 'Is there anything in your luggage you'll need? More suitable clothing, for instance?'

She regarded him thoughtfully, then nodded. 'I'll get a few things we may find useful.'

Savage watched her walk towards the baggage van as the sun began to sink. He screwed up his eyes. Something was moving in the distance: a covered wagon, alone, one family he assumed.

When Barbara returned, she was wearing jeans and a hat, stout walking shoes – Abbey's? he wondered – and carrying a small bag.

She looked in the direction he was looking. 'Think we might get a lift?'

'Could be.' Savage didn't fancy waiting with a bunch of passengers when the sun came up next

19

morning. 'Let's start walking.'

They kept going, one foot in front of the other under a sinking sun. The wagon seemed no nearer but, when he looked back the train they'd left appeared as a small scale model.

Barbara, he noted, once she'd adjusted her pace to his, had no difficulty keeping up. She hadn't always led a sheltered life, he guessed. They rested once for five minutes and sipped sparingly of their water. The sun reddened as it began to slip below the horizon.

Their shadows lengthened behind them, the wagon grew larger and it was almost dark when they came up to a fire with a pot simmering over it.

Savage hailed. 'Hello, the camp.'

'Identify yourselves.'

'You go first,' Savage told Barbara, and pushed her forward.

She glanced at him, but didn't argue: the smell from the cooking pot was tempting.

'Call me "Red",' she said. 'We're from the wrecked train.' She walked forward, into the fire-light. 'And hoping to get a ride with you.'

Savage waited a moment, then followed her, carrying his shotgun pointed at the ground. 'Savage. I'm a Pinkerton detective.'

The man behind the pool of light held a hunting rifle. 'George Jensen, farmer. You're welcome to eat with us, but we aren't taking passengers.'

'Don't reckon to be a passenger,' Savage said. 'I can hunt for the pot.'

His wife, a faded woman, gave him a weary smile. 'We could do with a change of diet, George.'

Barbara said, 'Your girl looks peaky, and I've done a bit of nursing.'

Jensen didn't appear convinced. 'We'll see. This is Martha' – he indicated his wife – 'and Helen.'

The girl was too thin and pale and Savage wondered what was wrong with her, but kept quiet. He squatted as Martha dished out stew from the pot. Barbara sat on a box. They ate hungrily and Martha said, 'Figure we can fit Red into the wagon tonight.'

Savage studied the wagon. It was not large, with canvas draped over hoops to keep out the weather, and likely packed with stores. Two horses, hobbled, grazed close by.

'I'll sleep underneath,' he said, unrolling his blanket.'

He wasn't long awake. He listened to the night sounds and watched the stars, wondering about Barbara Preston who called herself 'Red' and claimed to have experience as a nurse. Well, no kidnappers were likely to find her here. . . .

In the morning nothing was said about not taking passengers. Over breakfast, George admitted, 'We could do with some help along the trail. We're aiming to join my brother and his family – they're working a homestead out Cheyenne way.'

While George hitched the horses, Savage looked in the back of the wagon: a plough, tools, sacks of seed and provisions for the journey. It was a heavy load and they moved slower as the sun climbed higher. Savage walked alongside.

Red joined him, and didn't complain about roughing it. Neither did she show signs of impatience, despite a bridegroom waiting for her at the end of the journey. Martha, with young Helen, was up on the wagon.

Presently Savage saw antelope in the distance and borrowed George's rifle; he moved away at an angle so his approach avoided the wind carrying his scent to them. And returned three hours later with meat for the pot.

That set the pattern for the following days and, gradually, Savage roamed further afield. Sometimes Martha walked and Red rode with Helen.

One day, when Savage was out of sight beyond a distant rise, Red saw three riders approaching. She watched them closely and, as they came nearer, saw they were roughly dressed, unshaven and heavily armed.

She called to Jensen, 'Visitors.'

'I see them.' His voice sounded shaky.

The horsemen closed in, their hands filled with guns.

Jensen said, 'There's no money here. We're farmers.' He made no attempt to reach for the shotgun Savage had left when he borrowed his rifle. 'I've got two women and a sick child.'

'But you've got food and we're hungry. Stop, get a fire going and cook us a meal.' The leader was a tall and heavy man. 'The sooner you feed us, the quicker you get rid of us.'

Reluctantly, Jensen halted the team and turned the horses loose to graze. Martha and Red built a fire and added jerky to the cold stew in the pot. As soon as they began to eat, Red said, 'If you want money, take me with you. I'm worth your time – my father will pay well to get me back.'

'That so?' The big man didn't stop eating, but he looked carefully at her, uncertain whether to believe her or not.

The youngest one surveyed her figure with lust-ful eyes. 'She can double up with me,' he said. 'I won't mind an armful of that.'

Red smiled at him. 'D'you think you're man enough?'

'Cut it out, Luke,' the one with the scar grunted. 'We need to move fast.'

Martha said firmly, 'Leave the young lady alone.

23

She's not for the likes of you.'

Red returned her attention to the leader. 'My name's Preston, and my father owns a railroad. I bet you've seen his name in the newspapers, because he's a millionaire.'

The leader nodded. 'You're right, Todd – we need to move. But Luke can carry the gal if he wants – she could make a useful hostage if the posse catches up with us.'

The trio got their horses and Red climbed up behind Luke.

She spoke sharply. 'Let's get one thing straight – my father's old fashioned, and he's not going to pay for damaged goods.'

The three men and Red rode away from the wagon.

CHAPTER 3

HOSTAGE

Savage arrived back as Martha was preparing a meal. The wagon had halted early, the hobbled horses seemed skittish. George's face was pale and his lips a tight line. Young Helen was alone and looking frightened.

'Where's Red?'

'Gone.' George mumbled. 'It was her own idea – she volunteered. There were three of them, all armed. Desperate men, maybe escaped prisoners.'

'She offered to go with them, to save us,' Martha confirmed. 'She said her father was some bigshot who'd pay a ransom for her.'

Savage looked at George, who flushed. 'There was nothing I could do against them. They looked like killers.'

'So she took a chance, sacrificing herself for us.'

Savage smiled thinly. Maybe. Again he wondered about Barbara Preston who called herself Red: but it was still his job to look after her. It seemed unlikely that kidnappers could have tracked her here.

'Which way did they go?'

Martha pointed, and Savage sat with his back against the wagon, his legs straight out. He ate, then rested until evening. With moonrise, he took up his shotgun and a water canteen.

'You'll get her back, won't you?' Helen asked anxiously. 'I like her.'

'I'll get her back,' Savage confirmed, and headed out across the plain. A bright moon showed the tracks of three horses, one carrying a double load.

Red Preston had been feeling pleased with herself. That stopped when the one called Clay rode alongside her. He was the heaviest of the three and obviously dominated the others. He was the one who took decisions. Unshaven and smelly, he scowled at her.

'I saw your fellar go off hunting earlier – d'yuh reckon he'll follow us?'

'I'd say so. He's a Pinkerton, and he's paid to protect me.'

Clay slashed her across the face with his quirt. 'A Pinkerton!' The sudden pain told Red she'd made a mistake. 'Maybe we'll let him catch up – I hate those bastards! The law's bad enough, but that bunch poke their noses in just to make money. Yeah, it'll be nice to get one on his own!'

'Too true,' Todd added, and fingered the scar disfiguring his face. 'A Pinkerton did this, and I ain't the forgiving kind. Guess I can invent something slow and painful for this one.'

The young one laughed. 'Yeah, you two keep him occupied while I console his woman. She loses one man but gets me in exchange.'

'So keep moving along,' Clay growled. 'We want to be sure we really are in the middle of nowhere when we let him catch up, and not forget there's a posse somewhere behind us.'

Red felt dismay but hid it. She'd made a mistake: she'd have to shout a warning to alert him.

Luke's horse, carrying double weight, began to lag behind as the miles passed. When they reached the spot Clay picked for an ambush, Luke grinned as he let her down.

'You've got nothing to worry about, gal, 'cause I'm here to look after yuh.'

Clay spoilt this reassurance by knocking her to the ground. Todd tied her wrists and ankles, stuffed a cloth into her mouth and tied it in place so she was effectively silenced.

The horses were forced to their knees beside her and she realized they were in a dip in the ground and so out of sight.

Luke's gaze travelled over her body. 'Don't fret, gal. I'll give yuh all the loving you want after we fix this Pinkerton snoop.'

The gang settled to wait. Red stared up at the night sky and wished her face would stop smarting. She counted the stars.

Once he got his second wind, Savage began to alternate jogging with walking, a trick he'd learnt from an Indian he'd once worked with.

Cloud drifted across the face of the moon, making the light intermittent. Despite the apparent flatness of the land there were, here and there, bumps and hollows. After some hours, his scalp tingled as he approached a slight rise.

He'd learnt from experience not to ignore any warning, and slowed his pace and moved at an angle.

As he crested the rise a shot barely missed him. He dropped to the ground and rolled to one side as they came at him with a rush, cursing and shooting wildly. Three of them together, getting in each other's way.

Savage dropped his shotgun and drew his Bowie. Hands grabbed for him and he slashed out: the hands fell away. Something hard dented his Stetson, half-stunning him.

As he rolled, a voice cried out, 'Goddamn it, Luke, you hit me!'

Savage tried to curl into a ball but a smelly body elbowed him in the gut and his knife arm was pinned to the ground.

He used his teeth, drawing blood, and tried to wriggle clear. A heavy weight numbed his knife arm and he kicked out. He shifted one body but another replaced it: fighting one-handed against three thugs wasn't getting him far.

He was almost unconscious when a boot slammed into his side and a large hand grabbed him by the hair and jerked his head back. Flat on his back, he kicked out again but this time his legs were trapped and a rope noosed around his ankles and hauled tight. He was dragged over bumpy ground till he panted for breath.

Helpless now, his hands were tied and his Bowie picked up. The sharp point jabbed just below his eyes, drawing blood. Hands searched his pockets and took his folding money.

An out-of-breath voice gasped, 'Now we'll show yuh how we deal with Pinkerton spies!'

Another of them caught up his shotgun and

aimed at his stomach, finger on one trigger.

'Don't kill him easy – I want to make this one suffer.'

A hand snatched up his water bottle and emptied it on the ground. 'You won't need this any more.'

'You damn fool – don't you think we might want that?'

The one with the scar said, 'I'll begin to use the knife on him now, Clay.'

'There's no hurry, Toddy. Give him time to imagine all the things we're going to do.'

Clay Ferguson stood tall, surveying their back-trail. There were no pursuers in view, and that farmer sure wasn't going to do anything. He let the horses rise and graze.

'Start a fire, Luke – our hostage can cook. Toddy, help me stake this Pinkerton out.'

He slammed a revolver barrel across Savage's head, leaving him dizzy. He produced four iron tent pegs from a pack on his horse and hammered them into the ground.

Savage tried to put up a fight and got another belt across the head. He was spreadeagled, tied by wrists and ankles to the pegs.

Todd kicked him and spat in his face. 'You're going to die nice and slow, Pinky.'

Clay released Red, and hobbled her so she

couldn't run. 'If you cook real good, maybe we'll keep you on. Maybe.'

Luke poked at the fire and produced a blackened pot, strips of dried meat and cold beans.

Savage opened his eyes, and sniffed. His head ached and his mouth was dry.

Todd watched him and smiled. 'No sense wasting good food on a dead man.'

They ate, and Red was tied again. Todd produced a whiskey bottle, took a drink and passed it around. 'Don't call me early,' he said, and rolled into a blanket with his saddle for a headrest.

As the sky clouded over, Luke stared at Red and moistened his lips.

Red watched the whiskey bottle with approval. Men were easier to deal with when they were drunk. She had her gaze on the dying embers of the fire as Clay finally stretched out with a blanket and began to snore.

'Cold,' she murmured, and wriggled closer to the fire. Luke was watching her, but he was too young to be suspicious, his mind filled with his need for her.

In the starlight, her hand closed about a short stick a of wood that hadn't burned away: it had a splintered end, hardened by heat, and she slipped it inside her shirt. She waited.

31

It was not a long wait. Luke stood up and stretched, moving slowly towards her. She rolled away, towards the grazing horses. The sky darkened as night clouds hid the stars.

Luke followed, moving stealthily, not wanting any interruption from Clay or Todd. Red edged closer to the nearest horse, bringing out her stick.

When Luke grabbed for her shirt, she jabbed the hardened point into the horse's leg with all her strength. The horse lashed out with a snort and a shod hoof smashed into Luke's face. Red heard bone crunch as he went down: he went down on his back and didn't move.

One of the figures in a blanket stirred, but didn't investigate. The horse moved away. A silence stretched but Red didn't waste any more time.

She crawled towards Luke, his face soaked in blood, and explored his belt. He had a small knife in a sheath and she used this to cut herself free. She rose and stretched, then moved cautiously towards Savage.

His eyes were open, watching her with more than casual interest as she cut through the ropes spreadeagling him. Almost crippled, he massaged his arms and legs before trying to stand. When he could, he exercised for several minutes before feeling confident enough to take action.

Red followed him as he strode towards the sleep-
ers. Savage picked up his shotgun and checked
that both barrels were loaded, then kicked the
nearest body.

Scarface, half-asleep, reached for his revolver.
Savage triggered once, and Todd slumped back.

Clay stopped snoring, came awake, and froze.
Savage motioned him to get up and he obeyed,
slowly and carefully, looking around him.

'Unfasten your gunbelt.'

Savage stood back, covering him. He licked
parched lips. 'Water,' he murmured, and Red
passed him the bottle. One-handed, he drank
slowly, waiting to see if the gang leader would risk
a move.

When he didn't, Savage said, 'Get on your
horse.'

Clay glanced at Luke as he passed and Savage
watched carefully as he mounted up, bare-back.

'Start travelling and don't even think of turning
back!'

Clay Ferguson looked at him, memorizing his
face, nodded and set his horse in motion.

Savage stared after him till he was a speck on the
horizon as the sun came up, then faced Red.
'Guess you ain't quite helpless, so build a fire. I'm
starving. Bacon will do.'

She looked almost at the point of rebellion.

33

'First I rescue you, now I have to feed you. Will there be anything else, sir?'

'Not right now. I've a job to do and you're engaged to marry.'

Savage strapped on his Bowie, found his Stetson and collected all the water bottles. He searched Todd and found his own wallet.

'There's no bacon,' Red said, 'but maybe there's a reward for that one.' She indicated the horizon.

'Likely,' he agreed, 'but my job is to deliver you in San Francisco.'

After dried meat, beans and coffee they saddled the dead men's horses and headed west.

CHAPTER 4

'BRING OUT YOUR DEAD!'

'Why did you do it?' Savage asked.

They were riding side by side across the plain; the horses had been worked hard so they took it slowly.

'That's an easy one – I was tired of walking. They had horses, and I knew you'd follow.'

Savage nodded agreement: riding was certainly better.

'What I didn't expect was the hatred those men had for Pinkertons.' She made a face. 'Had you met them before?'

'Not those three, but others of their kind. Where there's no official law – as in the Territories

– we make it up as we go along.'

'I can see how they wouldn't like that – I was a bit of a rebel myself.'

'That so?'

The sun was now high and she took a sip from a canteen.

'My father insisted I go to a finishing school, and it wasn't all deportment and how to address the President's wife. Especially as I took advantage of the very different backgrounds of girls from other countries. I learnt a lot that wasn't in the official curriculum.'

Seemed there was something to be said for a finishing school, whatever that was, Savage reflected.

She smiled at some memory. 'We had a motto, "Anything a man can do, we can do better". The other girls used to call me Red Barbara—'

He glanced at the strands of flame-red hair straying out from beneath her hat.

'—before I was expelled.'

Savage started to force the pace. A natural loner, he was less than happy to act as nursemaid to a chattering female: and where the train had promised a swift end to this journey, it now looked like dragging on.

They made camp once before they reached the town of Ten Mile and rode along an almost deserted Main Street to the solemn *clanging* of a bell. Halfway along they reined back their horses and removed their hats as a funeral passed.

A wagon carried a small coffin with a family walking behind, heading for the out-of-town cemetery. The lone woman walked as if her legs had seized up, her face tear-stained. The street stayed empty, with only a few lined faces showing at shuttered windows.

Savage continued to the hotel, where Red dismounted. 'I'm not going any further until I've had a bath and a decent meal.'

'Can you pay for it?'

She ignored his remark, stepped onto the boardwalk and pushed open the door. 'Room and a bath,' she told the astonished hotelman.

He had a good eye and a patch over the other and seemed to regard her as one of the world's wonders. He leaned on his desk counter and asked, 'Are you aiming to stay in Ten Mile, ma'am?'

'Is there any reason I shouldn't?'

'People are leaving in a panic. This'll soon enough be a ghost town.'

'Why?'

'Folk are dropping like flies. It's the ague!'

Standing just behind her, Savage's scalp lifted. 'Let's go,' he said abruptly, and turned to leave.

'You can,' she said. 'I'm staying. Our horses need food and rest anyway.'

He hesitated a moment, and a memory came. . . .

. . . of a bitter winter in New York when he was still a child, a bare room with his parents stretched out in cheap wooden coffins. A hand pulled him away while the lids were nailed down.

'Come away. They're infected, and you don't want to catch anything.'

He remembered the long walk to the cemetery, the bell tolling, the gaping hole. One grave for two bodies.

The weather was damp and grey with a cutting wind and he shivered as the coffins were lowered. The grave diggers spaded earth over them as fast as they could. And then his parents were gone and a feeling of loneliness clamped about him like a strait-jacket.

A man in a top hat tried to lock him in an institution; he ran and stole food in a market. He slept in a warehouse down by the docks. He became a loner and learnt the tricks of survival, when to hide and when to fight.

He killed a man and ended up in Pinkerton's office with an offer that changed his life. It was all there, buried beneath the fear of disease, of wasting away, of a cruel and painful death. . . .

He shuddered and said, 'I'll see to the horses,' and hurried off.

He found a livery at the edge of town furthest from the cemetery and unsaddled the horses. A man dressed as a cowboy and spinning a lariat was the only person in sight.

'Will you feed them some corn in with the hay?' Savage asked.

'Sure will, boss. You want to pay me to learn to use a rope?'

'Not right now.' Savage was hungry, but decided against the hotel. 'Is there an eating place this end of town?'

'Sure is, boss. Give me some money and I'll bring back enough for two.'

Savage handed him a dollar and the lanky cowboy came back with tin plates filled with hash and a jug of black coffee. They sat in a relaxed silence as evening shadows came.

'Name's Evan, from Texas.'

'Savage. D'you work here?'

'Interesting question. I did, till the owner caught ill and died. I'm trying to get a stake together, then I'll be moving on.'

Evan paused to take more coffee. 'There ain't much to the cattle business these days, so I'm figuring to try the rodeo at Hangtown. A puncher can

39

sometimes win big money if he don't break his fool neck first.'

Savage had a worry nagging at him. 'This ague . . . is there a doctor here?'

'Only Doc Hennessy, and he's a bottle a day man.'

As the stable darkened, Evan rolled out his blanket on a layer of hay. Savage copied him, with the intention of collecting Red and leaving town first thing in the morning.

Red Preston was up early next day – a bell was ringing to announce another death, she washed and dressed and went down to breakfast.

One-Eye appeared to be on his own. 'I can do you pancakes and syrup – right now it's difficult to get supplies delivered.'

'Pancakes are fine,' she said absently. 'Isn't there a doctor in this town?'

One-Eye made a face. 'There's a fellar named Hennessy – trouble is he stays drunk as a skunk.'

Red frowned. 'Where can I find him?'

'About this time of day, sleeping it off behind the Star.'

She demolished her pancakes and went looking for the saloon.

It was easy enough to find, a large building with a false front near the centre of town. A star had been cut from a tin can and nailed over the door. A side alley led to the rear of the building where she almost fell over a body.

It was snoring and stank of cheap whiskey. This, she assumed, could only be the town doctor and, disgusted, kicked him.

An eye opened to regard her. A puzzled frown formed. 'What d'yuh think you're doing, Miss?' asked a blurred voice.

'I'd like to know that too,' Savage demanded, coming up behind her. 'It's time to quit this place.'

'You can, if you're scared. The people here need help and I'm going to see they get it.'

Savage regarded her thoughtfully. For a million-aire's daughter she was full of surprises. 'If this wreck is your only hope, there's a better way.'

He hefted the barely conscious drunk over his shoulder and carried him back to Main Street, to the horse trough outside the livery. He dumped him in and pushed his head under water.

The doctor struggled and spluttered and Savage kept pushing him under until he surfaced with some show of sobriety. His face was flushed and covered with a network of purple veins.

His voice shook as he spoke. 'Why can't you let sleeping docs lie?'

'Because there's a job to do,' Red told him, 'and I can't do everything myself.'

41

'We're leaving for California,' Savage repeated.

'You can. I'm not, yet.' She turned to Hennessy. 'It's time for your morning round, Doctor.'

'I need a drink!'

'Afterwards,' she said firmly.

Doc Hennessy, grumbling and dripping water, shuffled along Main to the school where sick children were stretched out, wrapped in blankets: then to wooden shacks where their elders lay waiting for deliverance or death. Some were hot and sweating with fever, some shivering.

Red shouted, 'Bring more blankets here!'

'There's not much I can do,' Doc mumbled.

'We can show that someone cares. That has to make a difference and—' She paused. 'Where does the town's drinking water come from?'

'We have a well.'

'Which may be contaminated. We'll boil all drinking water till this is over.'

The doctor held his head between his hands. 'My head. I need a—'

Red ignored him and went to find Savage. She found a cowboy showing him how to use a rope.

'Mr Savage, arrange for all water from the well to be boiled. Insist that no-one drink any water until it has been. Do that now. I'm putting you in charge.'

Savage stared blankly at her.

'I've followed my father all round the country while he's building rail tracks,' she said. 'I'm not inexperienced in nursing broken heads or fevers.'

He hesitated only briefly. It seemed he might get her away from Ten Mile sooner by going along with her. Assuming they both survived.

As she hurried away, Savage asked Evan to help. The cowboy was concentrating on lassooing a post, again and again.

'Boil water? I guess she means a whole lot of water. Waal, one time, before all this started, we had a laundry. They must have had something to boil clothes in.'

Savage went with him to investigate the laundry that was no longer in business, and found a large copper tub mounted above a wood-burning stove. Evan got the stove going while Savage persuaded some of the remaining townsfolk to provide a chain of buckets to fill the tub.

Some took a lot of convincing, but not all. One bleak-faced mother said, 'If this will save my boy, I'll haul water till I drop.'

Once the system was working on a regular basis, Evan dropped out to concentrate on his roping. 'I've got to keep practising for my big chance.'

Savage was interested: he always investigated anything that might prove its worth when survival was involved.

'How d'you do that?' he asked, gaining Evan's approval.

'I've got an old rope you can practise with. Let me show yuh how we rope steers at round-up time. Watch this.'

Savage watched, and then copied: and lassoed the post at his third attempt.

'Not bad,' Evan admitted, 'but hold it like this—' He demonstrated. 'Spread the noose – watch my wrist.' The lariat snaked through the air and dropped neatly over the post.

Savage imitated his action and lassoed the post first time.

'You've got it. Now it's a matter of practice. Just keep throwing that rope till the action becomes as natural as eating or drinking. Now I'll show you another trick. This is a way to stop a beef heading for the horizon – you cast the noose on the ground in front of the animal and, when it steps into the noose, jerk the rope up, so! And hold on tight and brace yourself 'cause if the steer doesn't hit the ground nose first, then you will!'

Savage looked at him. 'I don't think I'll be trying that one.'

The days passed as he mastered the art of rope-throwing until Red, exhausted but triumphant, came into the café and exclaimed, 'It's over. One of the seriously ill has recovered!'

She slumped into a chair and Savage brought her a coffee and Evan organized a meal.

She drained it at a gulp and Savage brought her a refill. 'I'm going to sleep for twenty four hours – then, if you still want, we can move on.'

'That's what I'm paid to do,' he said mildly. 'Get you to California.'

'Yeah, so it is. How could I have forgotten?'

Her attitude seemed altogether too casual for a young woman travelling to her wedding, some would say the most important day of her life.

CHAPTER 5

NO ROOM AT THE INN

'Hangtown,' Evan said with satisfaction.

Even Red Preston seemed interested. 'Do they let women compete?'

'It ain't usual,' the cowboy admitted, 'but I don't know of any rule against it.'

'And there's prize money?'

'You bet! That's the whole point as far as the competitors are concerned.'

Savage felt a twinge of alarm. Surely she couldn't be serious? 'That may not be a good idea.'

'On the other hand,' she said, 'it could bring in some cash, something I'm short of.'

As they headed along the old cattle trail that

split the town in two, Savage tasted dust. It drifted over the town like a permanent cloud and penetrated everywhere: maybe that was why there were so many saloons. Every other building advertised beer and hard liquor, and they were doing good business.

Further ahead, a crowd was cheering and Evan touched spurs to his horse. 'I'm doing to see what's doing.'

Savage glimpsed fences lined with cowboys and sightseers and, beyond, in a shroud of dust, a rider leaping high on a bucking horse. A banner proclaimed:

HANGTOWN RODEO

He saw corrals with horses and bulls and chutes leading into the arena. Further over was what looked like a railroad track and platform, and he made a mental note to investigate.

Red nudged his arm and pointed as they reached the hotel, a sprawling two-storey building with extra rooms tacked on. A notice was stuck up outside: *Rooms full: try our diner for the best steaks in town.*

'Steak sounds good to me.'

'Later.'

They hitched their horses, used a pump to refresh themselves and walked on to the rodeo arena, an expanse of dust that had once been lush green grass. People were coming and going all the while, buying drinks, eating sandwiches: it reminded Savage of a fairground back east.

Evan had started spinning his rope, trying to interest paying customers. 'Stand in for me,' he called to Savage. 'I'm going after the big money.'

Savage took his rope and began to spin it: only a small boy showed interest. Red said, 'I'm going to watch Evan,' and elbowed her way through the crowd.

Savage half-turned so he could keep an eye on her. It was not long before he heard a roar from the crowd and saw her rush forward.

Apparently Evan had been unseated by a bucking bronc and, as a result one leg was sticking out at an unnatural angle. He decided Red could cope.

His attention was distracted by a glimpse of a man in uniform: an employee of the railroad company, standing next to a man shouting bets. They were passing a bottle between them.

Savage pushed through the crowd and asked, 'Are the trains running again?'

The stationmaster wiped the neck of the bottle and offered it. 'The latest information I have is that the track has been cleared and relaid. Are you travelling east or west?'

Savage waved the bottle aside. 'West.'

'Tomorrow, around ten a.m.'

Savage relaxed; now all he had to do was to make sure Barbara Preston was on it. He coiled up his rope and moved their horses to a backstreet livery, to remove temptation.

When he returned to the arena, Red was watching a cowboy ride a bull. There was no saddle, and he clung to the back by a rope around the animal's body. Her gaze was critical as the rider came off like a missile from a catapult.

The contestant landed like a ball, rolling over and coming up running as men on foot darted in, trailing rags in the dust to distract the maddened bull.

He cleared the fence just ahead of the bull's horns and the timekeeper called, 'A good ride. He survived Rambo to a count of eight. Who's next up?'

There was a lack of volunteers. Then, before Savage could reach her, Red thrust her way to the front of the crowd. 'Me!'

After the briefest pause, the timekeeper realized this volunteer wasn't a cowboy. 'You sure?'

'I'm sure.'

'Hold that bull, boys. We've a gallant little lady eager to test her riding skills.'

Savage tried to stop her, but men got in his way and delayed him reaching her. The bull was

49

penned and Red hoisted high to land on the animal's broad back. She grabbed the rope with both hands.

'You ready, gal?'

'I'm ready.'

'Let him go!'

The gate of the chute opened and the bull shot clear into the arena like a ball from a cannon. She felt the great muscles under her quiver with fury. Rambo was a killer and wanted his rider on the ground where he could get at her.

The timekeeper was calling out, 'One . . . two . . . three. . . .'

The bull hit the fence across from the chute just as she jerked her leg clear; he ricochetted back into the arena to crash into the opposite fence.

Her teeth were rattling in her head. She heard cheers and catcalls from the crowd. 'Ride him, gal!' Head down, Rambo bounced off another fence.

'Four . . . five. . . .'

She seemed to have no air left in her lungs as she bounced up and down breathing dust. She heard the timekeeper counting, her hearing muffled and vision blurred. She gripped the rope as though it were a lifeline. His forelegs rose and came down in a spine-shaking smash. Then he dug his hoofs in and stopped.

Red sailed gracelessly over his head and hit the dirt.

Savage held his breath, but she knew how to fall; now where had she learnt that?

'. . . Nine!' yelled the timekeeper. 'A great ride from a great gal!'

But she was moving too slowly and four hundredweight of beef was ignoring those distractions meant to save her. Horns lowered, Rambo pawed the ground. Perhaps the dust helped, perhaps he couldn't see her clearly at first.

As he charged, Savage leapt the fence, rope in hand. He spread the noose and tossed it on the ground in front of the bull. The front hoofs missed, but the back ones were inside when he flipped the rope up.

The noose tightened and Rambo almost jerked Savage off his feet as he lunged for the fallen rider. Savage was dragged through the dust until a couple of other men grabbed the rope and hung on. All three dug their heels in, slowing the bull's angry charge.

They held on long enough for Red to reach the nearest fence, where willing hands pulled her over. Savage found himself alone, dropped the rope and vaulted the fence as Rambo turned on him with a snort.

'Nine seconds! The best today – is there another

volunteer to try to beat that? Nine seconds from a spunky gal. C'mon you guys, are you giving best to the only member of the fair sex to risk her neck?'

It seemed the men were happy to give her best.

'Red takes the prize money then.' The time-keeper flourished a handful of notes and coins and Savage collected her as she collected the money.

'That's it,' he said grimly. 'You've had your fun. Tomorrow we're on the train west.'

'Tomorrow? I'm concerned with right now. A meal, a bath and massage – I've got bruises every-where.' She looked at his hands as he brushed dust off. 'Are you any good at massage, Mr Savage?'

He smiled at the thought. 'Aren't you forgetting the hotel's full?'

'That won't be a problem now. If you'll find a room where you can double up, I'll take care of the rest.'

Savage shrugged. A room with a bed had its attractions after sleeping rough, and she had demonstrated her resourcefulness. 'OK.'

They walked to the hotel diner and she ordered steak and a bottle of wine. Savage drank cautiously. For the next few ninutes there was only the hum of conversation from the tables around them.

'That's better,' Red said, pushing away her empty plate and draining her glass. 'Let's see the hotelman – I'm beginning to stiffen up.'

The duty deskman nodded. 'There's one vacancy for doubling – fellar tried his luck at steer-roping and got unlucky. Doc's got him laid out in the barn he uses at rodeo time. Room sixteen, up the stairs and turn left.' He smirked. 'Don't imagine it will be the lady sharing.'

Red smiled sweetly. 'My mother warned me about strange men.'

Savage paid and followed her upstairs. 'Were you ever on the stage?'

'Only at college.'

He was beginning to wonder if she was always acting.

He pushed open the door of room sixteen. A cowboy, still with his boots on, lay on top of a single bed.

He opened one eye when he saw Savage. 'D'yuh want the window side?' He opened his other eye when he saw Red.

'Are you a drinking man?' she asked.

'I would be if I hadn't been cleaned out in a game of poker.'

She fanned a handful of banknotes in front of him and he sat up. 'What can I do for you, ma'am?'

'Find me a tin bath and fill it with hot water.'

The cowboy didn't even blink, but clattered

down the stairs to return with a galvanized iron tub. Savage sat on the edge of the bed watching as he returned with two buckets, a sliver of soap and a towel.

'Sorry, ma'am, but they won't allow any more hot water.'

'I'll manage,' she said, 'and I'll make you an offer. Whatever you win under fifty dollars, you keep. Anything over fifty, we split between us.'

She gave him his stake money and he went off whistling, winking at Savage.

Red shut the door and began to peel off. Savage propped a chair under the door handle to deter sightseers and returned to the bed to enjoy the show.

She had a solid body with breasts large enough to more than fill a man's hands, and wide hips. She eased herself into the water and sank down with a luxurious sigh.

It was some minutes before she began to scrub off the dirt. Already bruises were starting to develop and she towelled herself dry and said, 'Move over.' She lay face down on the bed.

'Now let's see what you can do. My arms feel as if they've nearly been pulled from their sockets.'

Savage bent over her, using his hands to knead her muscles. She murmured with pleasure as he continued to extend the massage. 'That's better

. . . and I admit I'm curious about that white streak in your hair!'

'Nothing much to it. A fellar took a shot at me and the nurse cut away some hair so the doc could get at the bullet. This is the way it grew back.'

'It gives you a distinguished look . . . keep going.'

Savage obeyed until she turned onto her back and smiled up at him. 'Now let's see how much man you really are.'

Savage could barely check himself. 'You're going west to marry—'

'Forget that nonsense. I had my first man while I was still at finishing school.'

Savage unbelted and struggled out of his pants, his need suddenly urgent.

She sniffed. 'Perhaps a bath first—'

'That can wait, I can't!'

He lunged for her as she spread her legs and wrapped her arms around him and held him prisoner until he exhausted himself.

But it wasn't Red Preston he saw at that moment, but the face of a dead woman: Bea, a school teacher murdered by mistake for himself. He remembered holding her in his arms as she died. He had pursued the murderer and killed him, but still her face haunted him.

Red murmured, 'That made me forget my aches and pains.'

Savage rolled off her and used the cooling water to wash down, opened the window and emptied the tub outside. There was a satisfying howl from below and he quietly closed the window and returned to their bed. It could be the start of a night to remember.

CHAPTER 6

SPECIAL DELIVERY

Savage let Red sleep late. He made a good break-fast and walked to the railroad and telegraph office.

'Yep, we're back in business,' the stationmaster confirmed happily. 'The line's cleared, track relaid. The next train west will call here in two hours.'

Savage showed his tickets, then walked to the livery. He indicated the horses they'd arrived on. 'What'll you give me for the pair?'

'Twenty,' the livery man said after a brief glance.

'Each?'

'The two. They've been hard used.'

'I'll chuck in the saddles.'

'Thirty, tops.'

'I'll take it.'

The liveryman peeled off notes from a roll and Savage thrust them into his pocket. He found his way to the doctor's surgery, a barn with stretchers or beds. The doctor was taking the air outside and smoking.

'You've got a fellar here calls hinself Evan.'

'Yeah, and he won't be going anywhere for a while.'

Savage handed him a ten dollar bill. 'This is money I owe Evan, and I'm just leaving town.'

The doctor lifted a bushy eyebrow in surprise. 'I'll see he gets it.'

Savage walked back to the hotel and went up to their room. He dragged the blanket off the bed. 'Better get dressed, Red. The train's due in less than two hours.'

She moved slowly, reluctantly, and took her time over breakfast. She was quiet, making no strong objection. They walked to the station at a leisurely pace and waited for the train as competitors and visitors gathered for the day's events.

The train arrived with a long whistle, a plume of dirty smoke and a clatter of couplings. A few kids cheered.

'Get off here for Hangtown rodeo!' bellowed the stationmaster, and many men did.

Further along the platform, someone was leaning out of a train window and waving. 'It's Nell,' Red said, and started towards the Irish maid she'd left behind at the train crash. Behind Nell, Dave was grinning.

Red and Savage boarded and Nell said, 'There's plenty of room in this coach. The compartment next to ours is empty. A lot of passengers went back to Chicago after the smash and . . . we're engaged! Dave asked me to marry him.' She winked at Red.

Dave seemed happy enough.

'Some story! The crash, and how people responded to it. I can hardly wait to get to Frisco to get it down on paper.'

Nell showed Red an empty compartment, and she nodded. 'It'll do.' She went in and Nell followed her, then Red shut the door in Savage's face.

Dave looked uncomfortable. 'Nell's been telling me a few things about Barbara that maybe you don't know. She's a reluctant bride, Mr Savage. Her father puts on an act of being wealthy, but he's not – he's an engineer who's spent his life, and a fortune, building railroads.'

Dave laid a finger alongside his pointed nose. 'He's about broke, and needs Crowther to back him – he hopes she can persuade her husband to put up the money he needs for his next project. Nell says, Barbara knows Crowther has a bad reputation and she's not keen on marrying him. So I guess she's just remembered what she's let herself in for.'

Savage shrugged. 'She's a big girl now.'

'All aboard,' the stationmaster called.

The locomotive whistled. The train eased into motion, gathered speed and headed for San Francisco; and Savage was left out in the cold.

On a fine Summer's day, Savage and Barbara Preston parted from Nell and Dave with a 'See you at the wedding!' From the railroad terminus, Barbara made a bee-line for *Blumfield's*, the first store she saw that showed the latest fashion in its windows.

Now suitably attired – Savage sported a new coat, Stetson and black string tie – they sat in a horse-drawn carriage travelling up Nob Hill to the mansion where Crowther looked down on the ants scurrying about below.

Savage's Bowie was covered by his coat, but he carried a loaded shotgun openly; on a previous visit, he'd learnt to be wary of the gangs of this city.

There was a short curved drive before the house, then steps up to a porch with carved pillars each side, and a bell-pull that jangled somewhere inside. The door opened to reveal an English-style butler.

'A delivery for Mr Crowther,' Savage said.

'Step inside, sir, madam, and I'll inform Mr Nolan, who acts for Mr Crowther.'

The man who arrived in the hall was handsome and affected bushy sideboards. He dressed the way a banker dressed and his manner was smooth as oil. A front man, Savage decided, noting the bulge of a hide-out gun.

'You're the Pinkerton, right? And Miss Preston – I've heard you were on the way.'

Nolan inspected Barbara from hair to pointed shoes, as if checking a banknote to make sure it was the genuine article. 'You're late arriving—'

'Our train was involved in a collision.'

Nolan frowned at the interruption. 'JC is busy right now, but I'll find out when he can see you.'

Nolan walked across the hall and Savage nudged Barbara to follow. As he opened the door into a drawing room, Savage pushed the door wide open and urged Barbara Preston inside.

It was a big room and expensively furnished. A comfortable room, where a man and a woman sat close together on a sofa.

The man came upright. 'What the hell d'you mean by breakin' in like this?'

Savage drawled, 'If you're Mr Crowther, I'm delivering your wife-to-be.'

The blonde woman stood up and smoothed

down her dress; a formfitting dress that revealed she had the form to fit it. She gave Barbara a glacial look.

'You forgot to mention you're planning to marry, Jerry.'

Crowther ignored her. He pointed at Savage's shotgun. 'You know I don't like guns anywhere near me, Albert.'

'He wasn't supposed to barge in like that,' Nolan protested.

'You're slipping.'

Crowther didn't impress Savage. He was small, and had that sly look about him that reminded Savage of a weasel.

The intended bridegroom took his time appraising Barbara, and seemed impressed by what he saw. 'Well, now that you're here, we must get to know each other.' He turned to the blonde. 'I'll see you later, Ruby.'

Ruby smirked. 'You bet your life you will, Jerry,' she said and stalked from the room.

'Your father, Barbara,' Crowther told her, 'like most easterners, is simply out of touch with real life. I'm no longer directly involved with any railroad, although I have money invested. I'm in banking now. That doesn't mean I'm not prepared to loan him money – at the bank's current rate of interest, providing he can convince me he – and the bank – will make a substantial profit. Of course I will.'

Savage expected Red to explode, but she remained calm.

'I don't believe that's what Dad had in mind. I suspect he expected a partnership, both of you sharing the risk, and the profit.'

Crowther shook his head sadly, as if sharing a risk was beyond his understanding. 'I think not.' He stared at Savage. 'But we mustn't bore *you* – you've delivered your charge and your job is at an end. You may go.

'Albert, see him off the premises – and a small tip will be in order.'

Savage nodded to Red and followed Nolan. At the door, Crowther's front man passed him a single banknote and shut the door on him.

As he went down the steps, Savage reflected on the end of a curious assignment. He wondered if there had ever been a kidnap threat: perhaps, perhaps not. More likely not.

Barbara Preston was no longer any concern of his, though he couldn't help wondering how she'd handle Crowther. She'd proved capable of looking after herself.

He glanced at the banknote Nolan had given before shoving it in his pocket. Ten bucks, a small tip? Well, he was in no hurry to return east, not without sampling what Frisco had to offer.

Red had revived his appetite, so he went looking for a high class brothel for the night.

San Francisco's Chinatown, after dark, was a maze of crooked alleys and shadowed doorways where anything might lurk. Near its heart loomed a large block of shops, houses and workplaces that appeared to be run-down; a tourist would have been surprised to find they were linked inside by passages and stairs and doorways that made up a second maze.

At the centre of this was a suite of private rooms that nobody was ever going to admit existed, and this was the lair of the leader of the New Dragon tong.

The main room was furnished in an eastern style and smelt of incense; the walls were covered by thick drapes to muffle sound. There were only two chairs: one a throne of red and gold on a subtly raised platform, where sat Mr Wu, current leader of the tong. Behind him was a screen and behind that a second door.

Mr Wu glanced over an ancient chess board with pieces of jade arranged in a problem. The other chair, the low one, was currently occupied by a small wrinkled figure whose great age commanded respect.

'Li Han, is my predecessor still obstinate in denying wrong doing?'

'Not entirely. I have obtained a written confession of many transgressions, yet I feel he can be persuaded to admit to more.'

'If anyone can, I don't doubt—'

A door opened to admit another Chinese. This one was huge and had the build of a wrestler with a shaven head.

He brought a newspaper which he handed to Wu.

'This latest edition of the Chronicle refers to the barbarian Crowther.'

Mr Wu inclined his head, then read in silence:

JERRY CROWTHER TO MARRY!
by Dave Merritt
Our Special Correspondent

Hot news straight from the bride-to-be!

Barbara Preston, daughter of the well-known eastern railroad promoter, Lew Preston, has arrived in San Francisco to marry the city's newest banker – spoiling the chances of many a hopeful beauty!

The marriage had been previously arranged between Mr Preston and Mr Crowther, and kept secret until now. A date and a venue have yet to be announced.

The Chronicle will tell all in a later edition. *Order your copy today.*

Mr Wu sat brooding and, when he finally rose to his feet, he made a tall vulture of a figure. His voice was deep and sombre.

'Li Han, you may dispose of my predecessor. You will soon have a new subject to practise your arts upon.'

He turned slightly to address the bald man. 'Kong, I wish to inspect this woman, Preston. Bring her to me.'

'I'm telling you I know nothing about it! Why can't you take my word?' Barbara Preston tried to remain calm, but her temper was rising.

Crowther slapped a copy of the *Chronicle* against his leg as he strode up and down the carpet. 'Because it puts pressure on me, that's why.'

They faced each other in the drawing room of his mansion on Nob Hill. Ruby reclined at ease, enjoying a cigarette and the row.

'My maid, Nell, became friendly with a journalist on the train coming here. It seems obvious now that she will have told him.'

Crowther still seemed doubtful. 'Maybe. . . .'

Barbara turned to glare at Ruby. 'And you can get rid of your fancy woman if you expect me to stay here!'

The blonde blew a smoke ring and laughed. 'You don't know JC if you think you're going to have him all to yourself.'

Barbara was not at all sure she was going to marry this man now there seemed little chance of her father getting the money he needed, except at a crippling rate of interest.

'He'll need to change his ways then. I'm going for a walk to cool down. So you think about what I've said, Mr Jerry Crowther!'

Red stalked out, blue eyes flashing, and slammed the door after her.

CHAPTER 7

WAITING AT THE CHURCH

'A visitor for you.'

Savage was surprised. Relaxing in the house's reception area, enjoying a small beer and chatting with the madam, he'd no idea that anyone knew or cared where he was. A few of the working girls lounged around in their underclothes, waiting for clients.

It was a superior house, clean and well furnished, and he'd enjoyed his brief stay: now he was thinking of returning east. Receiving a visitor was unusual and, at first, he didn't recognize the young man who was led to him.

Then he recalled him watching Barbara Preston

under the clocks at the railroad depot in Chicago and, later, pestering her on the train. A clerk, possibly, who wanted to marry her. Savage had lifted his ticket and left him behind at Omaha.

So he had perseverance. Savage studied him carefully and decided he might well make Red a more suitable husband than Jerry Crowther. He appeared tense at the moment, and Savage groped for a name.

'Abbey, isn't it? Boots?'

'That's right, Frank Abbey. And you're a Pinkerton detective. I need your help.'

'So sit down and take a drink – the young ladies won't bite. Maybe you can sell them some fancy shoes.'

A brunette brought Abbey a glass and he sipped cautiously. It seemed to Savage that this boy had grown since they last met.

Abbey asked abruptly, 'Have you ever met Crowther?' Savage nodded.

'He's a crook – so is Nolan.'

'Likely enough,' Savage agreed.

'Nolan visits this house,' the madam commented. 'And some of the girls complain about his little ways.'

Abbey took a deep breath. 'Barbara's disappeared. She left Crowther's place and hasn't returned – so he says.'

'She's a big girl now. I reckon she's capable of looking after herself.'

The madam shook her head slightly. 'Don't be too sure. There are parts of this city I wouldn't go alone.'

'Suppose we wait and see,' Savage suggested. 'Sell some more boots – give her twenty-four hours.'

Barbara Preston was feeling better by the time she reached the bottom of the hill. Away from the mansions of the rich, San Francisco appeared much like any other city she'd visited; a mixture of the new and the old, slums and building sites.

She doubted that Crowther would even offer to marry her, and her father could hardly expect her to force herself on him.

She remembered that Nell and Dave were getting married and decided to look for a suitable present. A street sign pointed to Chinatown and she thought she might find something different there.

She reached the Chinese quarter, where shops smelt of spices and perfumes and herbs. A narrow alley, filled with small shops, attracted her; she saw silks and birds in bamboo cages, good luck charms and exotic jewellery. Chinese words, painted in red and black, baffled her, but smiling bland faces offered goods for sale at modest prices. Music tinkled somewhere, but made no sort of tune she could recognize.

She was enjoying her window shopping until two burly figures pushed an elderly Chinese man against a wall in a threatening manner.

'Listen, Chinaboy, we want money. Regular money, ain't that right, Roo?'

Roo nodded. 'Yeah, regular, as in clockwork. You pay us and nothing bad will happen to yuh.'

'No savvy.'

'You savvy this?' Roo struck a match on the sole of his boot and held the flame under the elderly man's nose. 'Your shop burns to the ground if you don't pay us.'

Red was about to take a hand when a huge shadow detached itself from a doorway and blotted out the light. The man casting the shadow was a giant Chinese man with a shaven skull. He picked up the two hoodlums, one in each hand, and cracked their heads together with such force that Rod winced.

He dropped them in the alley, unconscious, and swung round to face her. 'You are Miss Preston?' He showed a newspaper with a photograph of Jerry Crowther.

'Yes, but—'

'My master wishes to speak with you.' The giant urged her into the shop as others appeared and dragged the two white men away.

Red was pushed through a doorway at the back of the shop, up a flight of narrow stairs and along a passage in semi-darkness. She heard sounds of life behind closed doors. A passage sloped down, then came two or three steps built on a spiral; she became aware of rooms at different levels. And still Kong urged her forward.

It was now obvious this could not be one shop. It reminded her of a warren, with links between buildings on the side of a hill. She stumbled on uneven steps and leaned sideways as a wall leaned. Sometimes a ceiling was so low the corridor seemed more like a tunnel.

There were shadows everywhere, whispers of sound, echoes: solid darkness in places and silence. The giant was behind her, guiding her with a firm hand when she hesitated. She never felt sure what was beyond the turning; more stairs up, more stairs down, a curtained doorway or simply another dividing in the main passage.

She knew she had no hope of eluding this giant Chinaman and, even should they become separated, she was hopelessly lost in a maze with no chance of retracing her path. They came to a corridor that ended in a heavy curtain.

'Wait here,' her guide said. 'Prepare yourself to meet my master.'

As he pushed past her and parted the drape,

light from within gleamed on a red and gold dragon. She waited, alone, in a perfumed twilight.

The sun shone. The bride wore white and the groom had a white flower in his buttonhole. The only cloud was a missing witness.

'If we wait just a few more minutes,' Nell pleaded, 'I'm sure she'll be here. She promised, so she must have been delayed.'

'I have another wedding in half an hour,' the minister said. 'I'm afraid I can't wait any longer. Besides, you have two other witnesses.'

Frank Abbey had come to see Barbara: and Savage drawled, 'Better go ahead, Dave. I don't think she'll be coming now.'

Disappointed, Nell agreed. The minister began, the minister's wife played the organ and they were pronounced man and wife. A few onlookers cheered and Savage got to kiss the bride.

The party adjourned to a nearby restaurant for the toast and wedding breakfast. The happy couple left for a brief honeymoon – Dave intended to get some background material from Nolan for an article he was preparing to write for the *Chronicle*.

'We'll have to take Barbara's disappearance seriously now,' Savage said when he was alone with Abbey.

Abbey nodded. 'I can get money from my family

to pay you, but it'll take time. I'm a clerk now because Dad believes I should learn the business by starting at the bottom, and gain experience in every department. But eventually I'll take over the business.'

'For now,' Savage said, 'I'll need something for operating expenses.'

'I'll telegraph my father right away.'

'OK. Then you go to the police because they've got the men for a large scale search.'

After Abbey had left, Savage took a cab up Nob Hill. He jangled the bell pull at Crowther's door and, when the butler answered, stepped briskly inside.

'We have an emergency and I need to speak with Mr Crowther.'

'Very well, sir, if you'll wait here, I'll inform the master.'

'Name's Savage. He's met me.'

'I remember, sir.'

Savage padded quietly after the butler and pushed past him when he opened the door of the drawing room.

'You again,' Crowther said, moving apart from Ruby. 'Can't I have any privacy? And do you have to carry that shotgun everywhere?'

'It's saved my life once or twice . . . I'm here to inform you that Miss Preston is missing and that her friends want to know if you've any idea where she is.'

'Hardly missing,' Crowther said casually. 'The Chinks have her – they also have an exaggerated idea of her worth.'

He fumbled in his coat for a crumpled piece of paper and offered it.

The blonde looked disapproving. 'You really ought to do something, Jerry. If it was me, I'd expect you to.'

'But it's not you.'

Savage smoothed out the crumpled paper to read a neatly penned script:

JC:

Delay in paying $20,000 will result in your bride being returned a piece at a time.

The only signature was a coiled dragon impressed in red ink.

Crowther laughed. 'That damned reporter's responsible, of course. It must have been his story that gave them the idea – so perhaps the Chronicle will start a collection for her.'

'You don't consider you have any responsibility for this?'

'Don't be ridiculous. I didn't invite her out here – and certainly I won't give money to a bunch of Chinese gangsters. I'd be laughed out of Frisco!

Besides, the Preston woman means nothing to me – let her father find the money if he wants her back.'

Savage folded the note carefully and slipped it in his pocket to show Abbey, and left.

Frank Abbey sent a message to his father from the telegraph office. He was not the sort of young man to chase young women when he should be working, and he trusted his father to respect his choice and understand that once married to Barbara he would settle down.

The telegraph operator directed him to police headquarters.

He made his way there, went up the steps and through the doorway. A desk sergeant regarded him without enthusiasm when he said, 'I want to report a missing person.'

'We get a lot of those in Frisco.'

Abbey didn't think his name would carry much weight here, but it was worth trying. 'Perhaps you're wearing Abbey boots? My family makes them.'

The sergeant stirred slightly. 'Not yet, sir. But if you have samples. . . ?'

'The name of the missing person is Miss Barbara Preston and, according to a newspaper report, she is engaged to Mr Jerry Crowther.'

'If you say JC's interested, then we are. Constable, have we had any word from him about this?'

'Not so far, sarge.'

'Then we'll need to wait till we get word.' The sergeant made himself comfortable again. 'You see, sir, we know JC's little ways. He indulges in a series of fiancées – it's off with the old and on with the new, so we can't really regard the young lady as missing, can we, constable?'

'Not unless JC says so, sarge.'

'Let me put it another way, sir, you obviously being new to Frisco.'

He made a steeple with his hands, as he'd once seen a lecturer do.

'In the beginning, there was a rush for gold. Then came the merchants and bankers, and they invented the law. A few, a very few – and hardly any of them miners – became rich, and they built their big houses up on the hill. JC was one of them – he made his money railroading – and Frisco today is run by the few up top. By and for, we might say.'

For a moment, the sergeant looked sad at missing his own chance.

'That's how it is, sir. If we hear from JC we shall scour the alleys and raid the houses, but it'll probably be too late by then for . . . what did you say her name was, sir?'

CHAPTER 8

BEYOND THE CURTAIN

Dave Merritt breezed into Crowther's bank and up to the counter. He was feeling good. Marriage, he decided, suited him. And as a featured special correspondent for the *Chronicle*, he felt he was on his way.

'I have an appointment with Mr Nolan.'

A clerk escorted him to the manager's office behind the counter and showed him in.

Albert Nolan gestured him to a seat. 'I thought I'd better see you myself to make the situation clear, as you're new to our city.' His handsome face clouded in a frown. 'Though the Chronicle should certainly have known better than to print such a rumour. Some days, one of these news rags gets above itself.'

'The forthcoming marriage is more than a rumour,' Dave told him. 'What I really need is some background material on Mr Crowther for my follow-up article.'

'Precisely my point,' Nolan said. 'Or to be exact, JC's point. I manage this bank for him, and arrange some other matters, as necessary, so you can take my word as official.' He lit a cigar but didn't offer Dave one. 'JC was disturbed by your article and has instructed me to make sure there will be no more.'

'The readers of the Chronicle are entitled to the latest news, and Mr Crowther's wedding is news. Our readers are entitled to know what's happening to people in the public eye.'

Nolan shook his head slowly. 'You're not listening to me. Your readers are not entitled to anything. Mr Crowther is entitled to his privacy; in fact, he insists on it.'

He blew on his cigar till the end glowed red, then stubbed it out on the back of Dave's hand. Dave howled.

'You maniac!'

Nolan drew a derringer and pointed it at him. 'I'm simply emphasizing JC's point. He's an important man here, and you're nothing. You can disappear in some back alley and no one, except your wife, would worry. Do you insist on making her a widow?

Dave stared at him. He knew that some gang bosses back east behaved this way; but a bank manager?

'Do we understand one another now? No more articles about JC.'

Dave moistened his lips. He'd never been at the wrong end of a gun before, his hand hurt, and he remembered that Barbara had disappeared. Suppose it was Nell who went missing?

'I suppose so,' he said reluctantly.

Albert Nolan smiled and the gun vanished into a holster beneath his coat. 'Excellent! I'll tell JC there's no need for further action. You can go now.'

The curtain was swept aside by a giant hand and warm yellow light revealed a room like a box.

'Enter.'

The walls were covered by thick drapes. Incense sticks smouldered. She saw two chairs with a chess set on a low table between them. There was a screen behind the throne-like chair where the giant's master sat: a Chinaman in a brocaded kimono.

Red Preston breathed in and strode into the

room, her gaze fixed on the figure on the throne. Stagy, she thought, and her lip curled.

'Be seated, Miss Preston.' The Chinaman's voice suggested an ancient culture.

She hesitated, reluctant to sit below the level of this man. She studied the board, allowed herself a tight smile and sat down. She moved one piece of jade and called, 'Check!'

He asked, 'You are Miss Preston?'

'That's me, and I bet you're not often beaten by a woman.'

'I'm not often beaten by anyone.'

He paused. 'And I suspect you recognize this arrangement of pieces as a chess problem. I find I do my clearest thinking while considering a problem. You may address me as Mr Wu. We are waiting for Li Han to join us.'

As if on cue, an old man shuffled from behind the screen; he resembled an insect, dried and shrivelled. Red stood up and offered him her chair.

Mr Wu spoke in a conversational tone. 'Li Han was chief torturer to the late Emperor. The present Emperor retired him, purely on grounds of age I assure you. His hand has lost nothing of its cunning. Stand where he can see you, please.'

Red blinked. She was not sure what she'd been expecting from the giant's master, but certainly not this. 'Why me?'

'I need you to persuade Mr Crowther to pay me a substantial sum of money for your return.'

'And if he doesn't?'

'Li Han will use his arts to convince the barbarian. Now Kong will take you to your quarters.'

Wu stood up, tall and gaunt, a brooding figure like a bird of prey wrapped in his red and black kimono.

'I regret it must be a cellar, but there you will not be disturbed – and if you can suppress your prejudice, you will find Li Han has many interesting stories to tell.'

Red had heard enough and was about to make a break for freedom when one of Kong's massive hands closed on her shoulder.

'Should you feel like writing to Mr Crowther,' Wu said, 'to encourage him to pay what I consider due, I shall see that your letter is promptly delivered. Between us, our efforts at persuasion will succeed.'

Savage felt the paving stones move under his boots. He stopped: a chimney pot crashed to the ground, missing him by inches.

A quiet voice said, 'It wasn't aimed at you, friend. That was an earth tremor, and locals ignore them. Obviously you weren't here long enough last time to experience one. We've met, remember?'

Now that his world had steadied again, Savage looked sharply at the man smiling at him: a dapper man, with a van Dyke beard and a silver-topped cane.

'It's Monty, isn't it? How's crime?'

'As ever – put one crook away and another pops up in his place. If you're staying longer this time, you may feel more than another tremor. Frisco is famous for its quakes.'

'I'm supposed to be returning east after making a delivery, but something turned up.'

Savage had been introduced to this city detective by a US marshal on a previous case, and they'd got on well.

'If its happening on my patch, I want to know about it.'

'I'll be glad to have your thoughts on this, Monty. Can we find a place to talk?'

'You bet.'

They strolled on together and Monty turned into a side street and pushed between double doors. The interior was shadowed and quiet with individual cubicles, each with high sides and backs to isolate them. Two cups and saucers were brought by a waiter, and coffee poured; there was brown sugar in a bowl and spoons.

'An advantage of living in a port is that some of

the best stuff stays here.'

Savage sipped cautiously, then nodded. 'I agree.' He explained the background of his latest assignment and showed the demand note.

Monty sighed. 'Crowther's a hard man to touch, and this tong leader is relatively new here. Most of the rackets are run by a bunch of Aussie criminals fleeing their own country. I hope we're not heading for a gang war.'

'I'm concerned about Barbara. Can you help me find whoever's running this New Dragon tong?'

'I can't, but I can introduce you to someone who may be able to help – a Chinese contact I have. Mostly, they're a law-abiding lot. After that, it's up to you. Most white Californians hate the Chinese and show it, so you won't find it easy to get one to trust you.'

They left the coffee shop and Monty walked him into the heart of Chinatown, to a herbalist's shop and introduced him to Cherry Blossom, a young and attractive Chinese woman.

She studied Savage carefully. 'I know you, Monty, and I'll accept your word for your friend. Perhaps Mr Wu will want to see him if it's about the American woman, perhaps not. Who knows? I shall send for Kong and he will decide.'

She called to a street urchin in her own tongue and the boy darted away.

'You will take tea with me while we wait,' she said, and showed Savage to a small table with two chairs in a corner of the shop.

Monty said, 'Keep in touch,' nodded to Cherry Blossom, and drifted away.

They sat quietly, drinking from dainty cups; the tea was light coloured and scented. All around them were shelves of jars containing herbs, charts and advertisements for massage, packets of green tea and vials of Red Flower oil.

There were bundles of incense sticks, each with its own perfume, and Savage wondered if she could tell one from another in the dark.

Kong arrived, impressing Savage. He knew he couldn't take this Chinaman; just the size of his bulging muscles was enough to show that. And his short-cropped hair, oiled flesh and loose clothing would make him hard to hold.

He guessed Kong had trained as a professional wrestler and to have any hope against him, he'd need speed and a trick throw.

'You come from the barbarian Crowther? You have brought the money for her?'

'No, I'm representing Barbara Preston. My opinion is that Crowther won't pay.'

Kong said in a flat tone, 'That is bad for Preston.'

'There are other ways of getting money. I need

85

to speak to your boss, to avoid unpleasantness.'

Kong deliberated. Cherry Blossom said something in a Chinese language. 'OK,' Kong said finally. 'Follow me if you choose to visit Mr Wu.'

He led the way past a curtain at the rear of the shop and up a flight of stairs. There was a passage with leaning walls and floors that were not quite level, doorways and bead curtains. They were, Savage guessed, moving between buildings in this twilight gloom.

He heard small sounds but saw no-one. Any member of the tong could apparently enter one building in the block and leave by another.

At one point there was an impressive suit of armour standing in a niche on a landing; one gauntlet grasped a heavy sword. It would take a giant to wear such armour and walk.

'Very ancient,' Kong murmured as they passed it.

They came to an embroidered curtain and Kong placed a large hand on Savage's shotgun; there seemed no way Savage could stop him taking it.

'You will get this weapon back after your interview.'

They passed beyond the curtain to a room where Mr Wu sat on his throne and studied a chess problem. Savage noted the draped walls – to deaden sound – and the throne sitting inches higher than the chair he was invited to use.

'I'll stand.'

'As you wish. Have you brought the money from Mr Crowther.'

'No, and I don't believe he intends to part with any of his money.'

'That would be unfortunate for Miss Preston. I am told you are a friend of the sergeant detective, the one who is not totally bigoted against my countrymen. As proof of our earnestness, I shall instruct you in the crimes of Jerry Crowther.'

Lamplight gleamed on a red and gold dragon; the smell of incense covered something less pleasant.

'I have come from our homeland to help my countrymen, exploited by the barbarian Crowther. He employed many Chinese in lowly and underpaid jobs, as miners and builders of his railroad. He has made much profit, which he does not share. Some of us have been injured and discarded, and their families need help. It is right he should pay ransom.'

'Sounds reasonable.' Savage admitted, 'except that Barbara Preston has nothing to do with it.'

Wu waved a hand tipped with lacquered nails. 'She is simply a pawn in the game. As she is his bride-to-be, he will pay to get her back unharmed. No man could do less.'

'I suspect Crowther aims to do a lot less. Nothing. But there are other ways of getting money from Crowther. I can help, but first I must see Miss Preston so I can assure her people she is still alive.'

Wu regarded him intently for a moment, then smiled. 'That can be arranged.'

CHAPTER 9

A MATTER OF MONEY

Lew Preston arrived in San Francisco dressed in his finest and expecting great things. When he left the depot he immediately bought a copy of a local newspaper. Then he hired a cab to carry him up Nob Hill to Crowther's residence; soon to be his daughter's home and so, he anticipated, his.

On the ride up, passing one great house after another, dreaming of the new railroad he planned to build with Crowther's backing, he searched the paper without discovering any mention of the forthcoming wedding.

He frowned and spoke to the driver. 'My name's Preston and I'm the father of the bride. Surely there's been some mention of my daughter's marriage to Jerry Crowther? I can find nothing in this rag.'

'Sure was, Mister, and the promise of more. I guess JC sat on that rumour pretty damn quick.'

'Rumour? Let me assure you—'

'Don't waste your breath. JC regularly dumps his latest fiancée for the next.'

'Does he? Well, he won't be dumping my daughter!'

Lew Preston stepped down from the cab and bounded up the steps to the front door. He jerked on the bell pull as if he were an invading army demanding entrance.

When the door opened, he pushed past the butler to the drawing room to confront Crowther; and found him with a blonde woman. 'Where's my daughter, damn you?'

Crowther raised an eyebrow. 'Who're you?' he asked coolly.

'Don't play games, Jerry,' Ruby said. 'Even I can guess this is Mr Preston. He deserves better.'

'Is she here? If so, I demand to see her. I want to know what's going on.'

'She's gone,' Ruby said, 'and if you want common sense, see Nolan at the bank. He knows most of it – Jerry's just not interested.'

'Bank? Knows most of what?' Preston was

getting worked up. 'Where is she?'

'She's been kidnapped,' Crowther said, and smirked. 'So now you're here, you can pay the ransom her kidnappers are demanding.'

'Ransom? What are the police doing?'

'The police?' Crowther laughed. 'You can try them, and good luck!'

Lew Preston sat down heavily. No wedding, and so no cash for his proposed railroad. Barbara kidnapped and a ransom demanded. He suddenly felt old.

Ruby poured him a drink and he swallowed it in one gulp. He struggled for control. 'This is your fault, Crowther!'

'No, Preston, it wasn't like that at all. Leaving here was entirely her own idea, but Ruby's right: you should see Albert, at the bank. He can arrange a loan for you.'

'A loan?'

'To buy back your daughter. I don't suppose you can raise the kind of money they're asking.'

Standing, Mr Wu should have been an imposing figure in his embroidered red and black kimono: tall and thin, his resemblance to a bird of prey was marked.

But Savage had met self-important people before, and wasn't impressed. He followed Wu from his sanctuary at the heart of the maze, along passages and down flights of stairs, and Kong followed him. They kept descending until Savage felt sure they were below street level.

They reached a door, barred on the outside, and Wu said. 'This is not a comfortable room, but it is safe. In this city of white barbarians, the best accommodation is denied to my race.'

Kong unbarred the door and Savage walked into a cellar. It felt cold and damp and he guessed the harbour could not be far away. The walls were stone, the floor bare earth and a single oil lamp burned; by its light he saw that Red was not alone. There was an old Chinaman with her.

Then he saw that Red was chained by one wrist, the other end cemented into a block in the wall. She appeared to be in good shape and looked relieved to see him.

Wu indicated the old man. 'The excellent Li Han. She is safe in his hands, but do impress on Mr Crowther that his bride has many removable parts, internal as well as external. I'm sure you can persuade him of the need to pay.'

Savage reached for the Bowie knife under his coat but Kong was ready and took the knife from him.

Wu smiled. 'So that your account will be as graphic as possible, you may view the first dismemberment.'

Kong tossed Savage's knife to Li Han and took a firm grip on Savage.

The old man tested the blade and expressed approval. The flame of the oil lamp flickered, making shadows dance on the bare walls. He stepped close to Red, and murmured, 'You will feel little pain if you do not resist.'

She glanced towards Savage, immobile in Kong's grasp. He shook his head slightly. 'This will also be the last time,' he promised her.

Li Han said, 'Please place your left hand on the block.'

There was a solid slab of wood on a small table, the sort Savage had seen in a butcher's shop: a chopping block.

'Excellent . . . fingers spread wide apart, if you will.'

The knife rose, gleaming hypnotically in the lamplight. It flashed down in one swift movement.

Red's face lost colour, but she made no sound.

'That wasn't so bad, was it?' Wu said smugly.

She looked at him storing every line of his face in her memory: this was one Chinaman she would surely know from all the others.

Li Man dipped the bleeding stump of her little finger into a yellow ointment, and Wu placed the severed finger in a small jewel box and handed it to Savage.

'Now you have a piece of her to convince Mr Crowther we are serious. Show him!'

Savage put the box in his pocket. 'You're making a mistake, Mr Wu. I don't think this will influence Crowther. Give me a little time and I'll show you there's another way to get money out of Crowther's bank.'

'Perhaps. We'll try my way first.'

Savage spoke directly to Red. 'I'll be back. Frank Abbey's here too, and he'll try to arrange something, I'm sure.'

Kong escorted him from the cellar.

Lew Preston was out of breath when he hurried into police headquarters. Since his wife had left him, he and Barbara had grown close; he was horrified by what Crowther had told him.

The desk sergeant sighed and waited till this visitor got his breathing under control and burst out, 'I want the head man!'

'Of course you do, sir. Can you tell me what it's about?'

'My daughter's been kidnapped by a Chinese tong, and I demand you do something about it now.'

'The name's Preston, is it? We know about that already, sir. Another man is with one of our detectives at this moment.'

'Another man? Who is he?'

'Constable,' the sergeant called. 'take our visitor along to Sergeant Montague.' He sat back with an air of satisfaction: another of life's little problems passed on to someone else.

Preston followed the constable along a passage, waited while he knocked and flung open the door. 'Mr Preston,' he announced.

Monty glared at him. 'Next time, knock and wait till I invite you to come in . . . please take a seat, Mr Preston. Do you know Mr Abbey?'

Preston recognized the young man as one of his daughter's suitors, and nodded.

The city detective said, 'I'm not going to pretend your daughter isn't in danger, or that Crowther's attitude isn't unhelpful, but finding anyone in Chinatown isn't easy. The Chinese keep very much to themselves and, unfortunately, have been treated badly by most of us, so it's not surprising they don't trust us. However, I do have one useful contact, and Mr Savage, a Pinkerton detective, is in there somewhere, searching for her.'

Preston began to warm to this dapper man with the pointed beard; not every police official co-operated with a Pinkerton. 'Savage? That's good.' And Abbey said, 'I agree.'

'I've worked with him once before, so I have some confidence—'

There was a tentative tap on the door and Monty smiled and drawled, 'Come.'

The constable opened the door and Savage walked in, kicking the door shut behind him.

'You have her?' Preston asked eagerly.

'No, but I've seen her. She's still alive.'

'Thank God!' Preston's face had been nearly as grey as his hair, but now he perked up.

'No chance of a raid, I suppose?' Monty asked.

Savage shook his head. 'Not a hope. She's in a cellar, in a block of buildings criss-crossed by internal passages. She'd almost certainly be killed before we reached her.'

'Damn Crowther!' Preston exploded. 'This is all his fault.'

Savage remained calm. 'We have to put Red first. Mr Wu, the tong boss seems quite serious. Look—' He opened the small jewel box to reveal the stump of Barbara Preston's little finger.

'He's started on her!' Preston shouted.

Frank Abbey clenched his hands. 'When I get hold of this Wu—'

'Let's all cool down,' Savage said. 'I've got an idea, if we can make it work.'

Monty stood up. 'I'll wish you good luck,' he said, and added before he left the room, 'If this involves breaking the law, I don't need to know. . . .'

Lew Preston moved briskly when he arrived at Crowther's bank. Savage's idea had changed despair to hope, and he had a role to play.

'My name's Preston, and I need to see Mr Nolan on a matter of business.'

'Yes sir. Please wait a moment.'

When the clerk returned, he said, 'This way, sir,' and showed him into the manager's office.

Nolan did not rise but regarded him with eyes as cold and hard as marbles. 'This is a courtesy maeting only, because of your daughter. Mr Crowther has already informed me that you are unlikely to have the security for a loan. Is that true?'

Preston kept his temper; he'd met men like this before: the second-in-command employed solely to do the dirty work. 'I'm appealing for money to help free my daughter—'

'A noble cause, some would say, but this bank exists to show a profit.'

Preston changed his line of attack. 'I'm also looking for financial backing for a railroad I propose to build between Frisco and—'

'JC has no further interest in the railroad business. Previously, the government guaranteed a fixed amount—'

'You're in charge here, I understand,' Preston

said sharply. 'How about you taking a decision? I never before came across a bank reluctant to make a profit. I have the experience – Crowther can't deny that – and if you put up the money, we split the profit.'

But it wasn't a railroad Preston was thinking of at that moment. A glint deep in Nolan's eyes suggested he had ideas his boss knew nothing of.

'When JC says "No" he means it!'

'So you're only the office boy. . . .' Preston kept talking while, outside, Savage leisurely circled the block.

He noted the condition of the stone walls and the iron gratings across the windows. There was a rear door to the bank and he tested it; locked and, he felt sure, barred on the inside.

He studied each of the shops near the bank, including one that had a TO LET sign outside. Of course there would be problems but, as he knew from experience, every problem has at least one solution.

He completed his tour and walked in the front door of the bank. There was no sign of Nolan; as agreed, Preston was keeping him talking.

Savage approached a clerk at the counter.

'If I were to deposit a weight of bullion here, do you have a secure vault?'

'Yes sir, we do. Allow me to show you.'

The clerk unlocked a door at the rear; beyond was a cage made of iron bars with a cement floor. The cage contained bars of silver and gold, and bundles of high denomination notes.

'Our working reserve, sir. Please observe that the lock has two keyholes: one key is held by Mr Crowther and the other by Mr Nolan, and they need to be used together to open it.'

The clerk smiled a superior smile. 'So you can see that your bullion will be safe with us.'

Savage nodded absently, working out in his head where the vault lay in relation to the back door around the block.

'Surely,' he agreed, 'and another day I'll arrange a time for delivery with your manager.'

He made a brief smile for the clerk and left; he took a cab up the hill to Crowther's place, not expecting much from the meeting, but he had to try for Red's sake.

The butler shook his head when he opened the door. 'I'm sorry, sir, but Mr. Crowther has given orders that you are not to be admitted.'

'Too bad,' Savage drawled, and walked past him and opened the door of the drawing room. Crowther was alone and he went in.

Crowther glowered at him. 'Can't you get it into your thick head that you're not welcome here?'

'I've something to show you.'

Savage brought the jewel box from his pocket, opened it and thrust it under Crowther's nose. 'This is the first instalment of Miss Preston, returned by the New Dragon tong.'

Crowther's face paled and he recoiled. 'I don't want to know. It's nothing to do with me!'

'All it takes is money. If you pay Mr Wu, we'll get her back with no more damage.'

'Not with my money! Oh no, she means nothing to me – just a bit of fun, that's all. I enjoy women too much to marry one. Variety is everything. I'd only marry an heiress bringing a fortune with her, and Preston is broke.'

Savage looked steadily at Jerry Crowther and decided to go ahead with his plan.

CHAPTER 10

QUESTION TIME

Clay Ferguson sat close by the window of a saloon, watching the passersby on San Francisco's Market Street. He had a gun, some money left from his last robbery and a price on his head.

He considered his next move with more than usual care. A bunch of Aussies seemed to be running the rackets here, and he was on his own. They were a rough bunch and he preferred to steer clear of them.

He bought another drink and idly watched the ladies of fashion in their carriages. A small man carrying a shot gun loped by, and he froze.

The memory of a face hovered, a face from the past, a face he intended to obliterate if they should meet again. He swallowed his whiskey and stepped outside.

He remembered Todd and Luke, himself being ordered at gunpoint to ride bareback into the wilderness, without a gun or water. He'd survived, only just eluding the posse on his trail. All because of some goddamned Pinkerton. . . .

A smile lit up his face: that Pinkerton was due a surprise. He remembered a name: Savage, and slowed his pace, just keeping him in sight. An easy target in a new suit coat and Stetson. Savage was apparently heading for Chinatown.

Well, that was dandy; there were alleys where a body would be ignored till the smell became too bad.

His quarry turned into a street filled with shops specializing in eastern food and clothing, then into a shadowed alley. Clay closed the gap; he didn't want to lose his prey now.

His pursuit was so concentrated he didn't realize he had an interested audience until a bunch of toughs surrounded him.

'Not so fast, big boy,' came a voice with a harsh accent. 'I've a few questions for you.'

Reluctantly. Clay stopped. He guessed these were some of the Aussies he didn't want trouble with, but Savage was getting away.

'I'm with you,' he said quickly. 'Let me go and

I'll rid you of a Pinkerton.'

'Private, is he? So you do have things to tell us. Come quietly now. It seems he has some kind of deal on with the Chinks, and that interests us.'

For a moment, Clay was tempted to break away, but the Aussie boss, a small man, said, 'We can hand you that one on a plate any time, 'cause we know where he hangs out. You help us, we help you.'

Clay realized Savage had already disappeared, and made an effort to relax. 'OK, we'll do it your way.'

'That's right,' the small man said flatly, 'my way. Come along with us and we'll have a quiet drink and a chat. Just keep in mind I've killed bigger men than you without much trouble.'

Clay didn't think he was boasting: his skin looked as tough as leather.

The gang didn't hurry, but people moved out of their way as they headed down to the waterfront. There was a smell of tar and fish; boys chased rats for sport. Ships, some with tall masts, filled the bay. A little way along the shore from the moorings a saloon stood on its own.

The *Shamrock* announced a signboard, and the Aussies walked in as if they owned the place.

A small woman with vivid orange hair glared at them from behind a counter. 'If you're aiming to

103

make this one talk,' she snapped, 'clear out. I'm tired of washing out bloodstains after you lot.'

'Keep your hair on, Irish. My friend is just here for a friendly exchange of views.'

'Make sure it stays that way, Bruce.'

The gang herded Clay to a corner table and sat down. Irish brought a bottle and glasses. 'I suppose you're paying, friend.'

'I suppose I am.' Clay paid, and Bruce poured. 'Cheers, mate. What name are you using?'

'Clay.'

Bruce drank slowly, watchful. 'So, Clay, what d'you have to tell me? About this Pinkerton to start with, then anything else that occurs to you. Information is one thing I can never get enough of. It's my life blood so to speak.'

Clay took a swallow of whiskey. 'I was out west with a couple of good old boys when we came across this wagon. There was a gal with it, name of Preston, who claimed her father was rich, so we took her along for insurance. At that time, you understand, we had the law nipping at our heels.'

Clay licked his lips, suddenly dry, and poured himself another drink.

'It turned out she had a Pinkerton to guard her but he was off hunting, and came after us. We had a bit of a skirmish and both my mates were killed and I was left in the middle of nowhere without a gun or water. So you can see I owe him.'

'Preston,' Bruce said, looking thoughtful. 'That name's been in the papers, but the story I heard is her old man's poor as a church mouse.'

Another of the Aussies – this one had a bandaged head – added, 'The grape-vine says the Chinks have her now, and that makes me wonder—'

'I want the Pinkerton!'

'Sure, Clay,' Bruce said easily. 'But I reckon to ask him a few questions first. Like, what's he up to with the Chinks, because it seems to me they're trying to take over our rackets. When I've got answers, then you can have him to play with.'

Savage returned to the herbalist's shop and this time there was no delay. Cherry Blossom smiled and bowed a welcome; he didn't see her signal, but Kong appeared remarkably quickly.

Their journey to the room at the heart of the maze was still one of ups and downs, steps and slopes, dark corners and silent doorways, but seemed shorter than before. Savage guessed this was a more direct route. They passed the giant suit of armour and then the dragon curtain was swept aside and he entered Wu's inner sanctum. At least this inscrutable Chinaman didn't pretend to despise money.

This time Savage sat down, with Kong standing behind him. The chess board on the table had been removed. The tong leader, seated on his throne, clapped his hands and, from behind the rear curtain came a young Chinese woman bearing a tray with cups, saucers and a tea pot. She poured for them and went out and Wu asked, 'Crowther will pay?'

Savage let him wait while he sipped the tea; it was not to his taste and he put down the cup.

'Not a cent. He denies responsibility.'

'Unfortunate for Miss Preston.'

'But not necessarily for you.' Savage was aware of Kong breathing down his neck. 'I have a plan to clean out Crowther's bank, and that will surely produce more than you're asking. Of course, there'll be expenses, but they shouldn't worry a man controlling unlimited labour. Are you listening?'

'I'm listening.'

'Miss Preston's father is an engineer and he'll be in charge. You'll provide men with experience in mining. I'll keep Crowther and Nolan out of the way. Can you provide a show of fireworks at the critical moment, as a distraction?'

'That should prove easy enough. One of my members owns a fireworks factory.'

Wu listened closely as Savage went into more

detail. At the end, he nodded.

'Indeed yes. Mr Savage, your plan has my approval, and I foresee good fortune and a successful outcome. Start at once and keep me informed each step of the way.'

'Then I'm formally asking you to release Miss Preston.'

Wu gave him a bland smile. 'Not until I have the money from Crowther's vault securely in my possession. But I give my word she will be well treated and that no harm shall come to her.'

Mr Wu sipped delicately at his tea. 'Most refreshing. Remember, the sooner you succeed, the sooner I shall be able to release her.'

'I'll need to see her—'

'That will not be necessary. I shall assure her myself that the moment you deliver the contents of Crowther's vault, she will be released unharmed.'

Savage stared at the tong boss, wondering if he should say anything. He decided not. It didn't seem to have occurred to Mr Wu that Red might have something else in mind than leaving quietly.

After Savage left, he made his way by the most direct route to Dave and Nell's second floor apartment for a meeting with others of the rescue party.

The apartment had been nominated headquarters because one big window gave a view overlooking the front entrance to Crowther's bank. Equipped with binoculars, they each took a turn timing the comings and goings of Nolan and his head clerk.

Savage's mind was on organizing the next step in his plan. He needed to talk to Lew Preston, the only one of them with any practical experience. Deep in thought and hurrying along the sidewalk, the attack took him by surprise.

A hand grabbed his arm before he could raise his shotgun to firing position, at the same moment, the point of a knife touched the back of his neck and a foot tripped him.

Savage didn't hesitate: he dived forward, head tucked in and rolling sideways, dragging one attacker with him and damaging another as he lashed out with his boots.

'Bloody hell,' bawled a voice with an Australian accent. 'Knock the bastard out – we'll have to carry him.'

For an instant, Savage caught a glimpse of a small man with a skin like tanned leather. Passersby scattered as Savage freed his Bowie and lashed out. A man cursed. Someone trod on his knife arm, numbing it – he recognized Clay, the big leader of the outlaws who'd grabbed Red from the wagon on their way to Frisco.

He slammed a balled hand into Clay's throat,

then more bodies piled on top of him. Clay choked on his last words, 'This is for—' and toppled forward across him, spraying blood like a fountain.

Suddenly it seemed as if the gang of Aussies was surrounded by twice as many small yellow men each wielding hatchets. They chopped at their bigger opponents like lumberjacks felling trees. For a long moment, the street was apparently the scene of a race riot, then both the Aussies and Chinese melted away, taking their wounded with them.

Savage came up for air, limping, bloody and bruised. It felt as if an elephant had been standing on his stomach, and it took a while to get his breathing under control. He collected his shotgun and Bowie and checked both.

Clay and one Aussie lay lifeless and Monty stood over them, prodding at the bodies with his cane. He regarded Savage with disapproval.

'While I applaud the reduction of our criminal element, I thought I'd mentioned I don't need a gang war on my turf?'

'I'm sure you did, but I don't see why they picked on me.'

'You've been meeting with the Chinese, and Bruce won't like that. Figure he wanted to teach you a lesson.'

And Wu's protecting his investment, Savage thought; he's taking this bank job seriously. He smiled, pleased with the way things were shaping.

Lew Preston was unhappy. He stared through binoculars from the window of Dave and Nell's apartment at the front entrance of Crowther's bank. He was supposed to be noting down the times of Nolan's comings and goings.

He saw nothing, his mind clouded by the past, dwelling in a time before he switched from mining to railroads. Mostly he could forget the past, but this job brought it back.

It was not a time he was proud of, and he'd never told Barbara about it.

He felt almost physically sick. Caught without money, his daughter at risk – no thanks to Jerry Crowther – and now forced to return to his role as mining engineer, a career he only wanted to forget. Yet he had to do it for her sake.

Usually remembered only in his worst nightmares, he relived the time when men had died underground because he'd made a single mistake, a simple error of which he was ashamed. When the explosion came and he realized what he'd done, he'd panicked and bolted. He had survived where others had not. He'd been young then, but still. . . .

Behind him, a door opened and Savage limped in, looking the worse for wear.

Dave looked up from his writing. 'What happened?'

Nell bustled up, bringing hot water and bandages, and not about to be put off. 'It's important not to get dirt into an open wound. You must keep it covered till the skin heals over.'

Dave tipped brandy into black coffee, haunted by a feeling of guilt, blaming himself for Barbara's kidnapping.

After Savage had told his story, Frank Abbey asked, 'Will this change Barbara's situation?'

Savage shrugged. 'Who knows?'

'I don't feel I'm doing much,' Abbey said. 'So far, just putting up the rent for the shop we'll be using. I'd like a gun for when we break in.'

'Have you ever fired a gun?'

'Only on a target range.'

'Did you hit anything?'

'Nope.'

'See this?' Savage broke open his shotgun and took out two shells, pushed them back in and closed the gun. 'As easy as that – just point and pull the trigger. It might not be necessary to fire at all – some fellars don't like having a shotgun pointed at them at close range.'

'I'll buy one and practice.'

Savage turned to Preston. 'Have you looked over the shop yet?'

The engineer nodded. 'It'll do. The job will take time, but we can do it.'

'Will you need explosives?'

'Good God, no! Apart from the noise giving us away, the ground here is unstable. No, this job has to be done the hard way, using men with picks and shovels, buckets and barrows.'

'You're the boss.'

Preston nodded, accepting responsibility.

'I'll stick up a builder's sign as cover and start a rumour about the new shopkeeper wanting alterations.'

'Fine.' Savage looked around a ring of anxious faces. 'I have to say I wasn't expecting trouble from another quarter, so the sooner we make a start the better.'

CHAPTER 11

THE TUNNEL

'Stone walls do not a prison make,' muttered Barbara Preston, 'but they surely make a cold, damp cellar.'

Li Han surveyed her without a smile as she once again jerked uselessly at the chain securing her to the wall.

'You must learn patience, Miss Preston.' The old Chinese seemed right at home living down here, she thought.

'Guess you're right,' she admitted. 'I've learnt all kinds of things in my life, but never that. It looks like I'll have time to learn now as no one seems in a hurry to rescue me.'

'I'm sure your friends are doing their best to raise the money for your release.'

'I suppose so – it's just that time drags.'

She wondered how Nell and Dave were getting on; she'd been looking forward to the party after their wedding. Had they found a place to live? Did they know why she'd failed to arrive at the church?

Savage had promised to return, and she had some confidence in him, but he was taking his time. Her finger throbbed and, sometimes, it was hard to ignore; how could she feel what was no longer there? She'd heard of phantom limbs troubling amputees, but this was ridiculous.

Frank Abbey had followed her to San Francisco, apparently; maybe she would marry him if—

'Shall I set up the chess pieces again?'

'Why not? It'll pass the time, and I might get to beat you one day.'

She studied the old man thoughtfully; he looked harmless enough.

'How d'you ever get to be chief torturer? I wouldn't have thought there was a queue for a job like that.'

'It is a hereditary position, and I was trained from infancy. It is an honourable profession. though I do not expect a barbarian to understand.'

'Not so much of the barbarian, if you don't mind. Some folk think torture is pretty barbaric.

You start off this time, so you can make the first mistake.'

Li Han smiled faintly. 'If you are waiting for me to make a false move, you will indeed need to learn the art of patience.'

'Maybe.' She brought out a knight to counter his opening pawn.

She didn't blame the old man: he obeyed orders, but Mr Wu was a legitimate target. Past times with Dad, on the move and short of money, had been rough, but nothing like this. Where was Dad anyway?

When it came to Mr Wu however, she could be as patient as a cat waiting at a mousehole.

Lew Preston had already begun to sweat. He tried to stay calm, telling himself it was only a few feet below ground; nothing to a mining engineer.

But memory was stronger than mere thought, and went on insisting there was danger. He stared at the hole knocked in the wall of the cellar below the shop Abbey had bought. The Chinese provided by Wu's New Dragon tong had already started tunnelling and he didn't want to go in there. He really didn't – his mouth was dry and his legs trembling – but he had to, to help Barbara.

He took a deep breath, bent over and crawled

inside. An oil lamp showed they hadn't got far as yet, and he saw that the roof was crumbling.

'Pit props,' he ordered. 'Shore up the roof before you go any further. And keep shoring every five yards.'

He withdrew then; while he concentrated on detail he could cope. In the past, he'd used a pidgin English to communicate with his workers. This time Wu had supplied a translator whose English was correct, but stilted.

Work stopped while men brought in timber from outside, and the translator regarded him with open curiosity.

'You are ill, sir? Should I summon a doctor?'

Preston shook himself. 'There's no need. I once had a bad experience and lost men – but no one dies on this job.'

These men, it was obvious, had been previously employed as miners. As soon as they propped up the sagging roof, Preston practised deep breathing to calm his nerves and then crawled to the far end of the tunnel.

He realized that digging was not a problem; it was the time taken to clear the earth and rubble that would delay them.

'OK, carry on,' he said, 'while I figure out a way to shift this stuff quicker.'

Shaking, he backed into the open, mumbling to

116

himself; 'A flat trolley, four small wheels and a rope to pull it. . . .'

Savage was bored. Now that Preston had taken charge of the main job, he was taking his turn at the apartment window, watching Crowther's bank, and nothing much was happening.

His injuries were healing and his mind wandered, searching for a more active role to play: waiting did not come easily to him.

When his attention returned to the front entrance of the bank, Nolan was just coming out with another man. One he recognized from the street fight: a small man with a leathery skin.

Monty had identified him as Bruce: so what was the Aussie gang boss doing with Crowther's bank manager?

Well, it didn't matter. His brain raced. What mattered was that this situation could be used to spark dissension between the bank's owner and his manager.

'Dave,' he called. 'Take over here, will you? I've an errand to run.'

The journalist had finally gotten down to writing up his railroad trip.

'You're not fit enough yet,' Nell said.

'I'm only going to talk to a man.'

Outside he hired a cab to take him up the hill,

but this time he didn't have to force an entrance. As he arrived, Crowther and Ruby were leaving in an ornate carriage, going downhill.

'Turn around,' Savage told his driver. 'and follow that carriage!'

Going down went faster than coming up and, in a short time, his quarry drew up outside Bluefield's, the ladies fashion store that Barbara had visited when she arrived in San Francisco. Crowther and Ruby disappeared inside; Savage paid off his cab and followed.

Discreet notices indicated Crowther's interest: *The latest designs from Paris, France: Ladies underwear and nightwear.*

The fashion show was being staged in a separate room, curtained off and with a porter at the entrance. He passed Crowther and Ruby, but stopped Savage.

'I've an urgent message for Mr Crowther, and have only just caught up with him.'

He slipped the porter a dollar and passed through. There were three rows of chairs and Crowther and Ruby sat in the middle of the front row. The audience consisted mainly of wealthy men with young ladies; not their wives, Savage surmised.

Young girls paraded before the audience wearing camiknickers and frilly nightdresses while a tall and elegant woman introduced each model in turn:

'. . . now wearing Directoire knickers . . . for the fuller figure with matching garters . . . this daring little number we call "Honeymoon Nights". . . .'

The chair next to Crowther was vacant, and Savage slid into it. Ruby seemed at ease here; maybe she'd been one of the store's models. Maybe this was where Crowther obtained his fiancées.

Ruby spotted him first and nudged Crowther, who frowned.

'You again – don't you ever quit?'

Savage made a smile and whispered, 'Doing you a favour, JC. Your man Nolan is partnering that Aussie gang boss – you can guess what that means.'

'Even an Australian is entitled to pay money into my bank.'

'But has he? Has Nolan told you so?'

Crowther's lip curled in contempt. 'You're just trying to make trouble.'

'Why should I do that?' Savage managed to sound puzzled.

Ruby said, 'I never trusted that Nolan. Maybe you should investigate, Jerry.'

'There's no need. I trust Albert. . . .' Crowther's voice faded away. A seed had been planted. Savage got up, nodded to Ruby, and left the store.

Bruce sat quietly, thinking. It was his ability to plan ahead that enabled him to control his gang.

The other Aussies were drinking hard and talking violence: Roo, his head still bandaged, was loudest of all.

'I want to get Kong, and I say we should burn the Chinks out. Start a real blaze going in Chinatown and loot the shops when they run – if a few slit-eyes end up dead, who's going to worry?'

It seemed the whole gang was in favour. The *Shamrock* reverberated with noise and Irish watched them, ready to take physical action if it looked like a riot was starting. She tapped on the counter with a cut-down billiard cue.

Bruce frowned. 'Calm down, you blokes. We've got a job that comes first.'

Roo snarled, 'Who says? My head still hurts and I want to even the score.'

'What's this job then?' cut in another of the gang.

'If you'll use your ears instead of your tongues, I'll tell you.'

The noise lessened and Bruce spoke in a low voice. 'I've had words with Nolan, at Crowther's bank. He reckons he's ready to take over, and wants us to take care of Crowther for him. Seems

JC's too keen on the sheilas and neglects business.'

'I never figured Nolan for a double-crosser.'

'So now we know what to expect. He uses us, so he'll find we can lean on him. Sounds good to me.'

'Crowther's got a lot of clout,' Roo objected, 'and it sounds dodgy to me. We do what Nolan wants and he drops us right in it. I still say, let's gut Chinatown and kill Kong!'

Bruce looked hard at him. This was the first time any member of the gang had dared to challenge his authority.

CHAPTER 12

THE SECOND TEAM

Frank Abbey looked older and held his newly acquired shotgun as if he knew how to use it.

Monty said, 'Never point a gun at a man unless you're going to use it.'

He didn't know whether to laugh or cry. This easterner had been a joke at first but, fired with a determination to reach the woman he intended to marry, he looked capable of starting a one-man war.

Monty wasn't sure he approved. He was in favour of eliminating criminals, but in a manner acceptable to the law. And Savage, sketching a map on his desk, in his office, a map showing the internal route from a herbal shop to where he suspected Miss Preston's prison might be, positively alarmed him. The Pinkerton apparently expected him to go along on this crazy rescue mission.

'It was you who said reaching her was impossible,' he objected.

'True.' Savage dropped a stub of pencil on his desk. 'But that was before Frank said he was going it alone.'

'So he'll fail.'

'Likely you both will. But it'll make another diversion and help confuse the situation. I don't entirely trust Mr Wu, and this gives us a chance to keep him off balance.'

'Let's not forget this tong is just another bunch of crooks as far as I'm concerned.'

'Let's not forget Miss Preston has been kidnapped and held for ransom. Some people night think the police should take a bit more interest.'

Monty sighed. His office was small and cramped, the walls covered by 'Wanted' notices. He had long ago learnt that he couldn't win no matter what he did.

'I just want to get her out of there,' Abbey said.

'I can sympathise, but—'

Someone knocked on his door and Monty called, 'Come.'

A policeman looked around the edge of the

door. 'Mr Savage, we've had a message from JC. He wants to see you.'

'Interesting.' Savage smiled like a wolf. 'I somehow doubt he's had a change of heart, so . . . keep me posted, Frank.'

He nodded to Monty and went out.

'A pleasure to welcome you, sir,' murmured Crowther's butler. 'You are expected this time, so this way if you please.'

Savage was led to a small study. There was a desk, comfortable chairs and a table with bottles and glasses. From here, Savage assumed, Crowther ran his financial empire.

JC was alone. 'A drink?'

'I'm not much of a drinking man.'

'Take a seat then. We've things to discuss and I have a proposition to put to you.'

Savage sat, alert, and Crowther poured a large brandy for himself; he looked as if it wasn't his first today.

'I've been considering your suspicions about Albert, and I suspect you're right. I'm disappointed in him. He's no good on his own and I really thought he had more sense.'

'Then you'll put up the money for Miss Preston?'

Crowther frowned. 'Of course not! Forget her – she's not important.'

'Then I don't see we have anything to discuss.'

'You really must learn to put your own interests first, Savage, or you'll never get anywhere. I made a fortune out of the government – they wanted a railroad built and paid a fixed price for each mile of track. I didn't let anything stop my crews laying track. That fortune gave me my start in banking – and, again, I'm not about to let anything stop me making a second fortune, so do yourself some good and listen. . . .'

He took another swallow of brandy. 'I want to hire you as my personal bodyguard, to protect me from Nolan's Aussie criminals, or whoever, and I'll pay well.'

Savage's thoughts raced. This was not what he'd been expecting, and he quickly considered the idea. It would give him the chance to get close to Crowther and keep an eye on him during the run up to the bank job.

'And Nolan?'

'Nolan can wait till I've trained a suitable replacement. Then you can kill him.'

You cold-blooded devil, Savage thought, and asked, 'How much?'

'Fifty a month for as long as necessary.'

'One hundred.'

'Agreed.' Crowther smiled, sure he had got the best of the bargain.

125

*

The house was lower down the hill and Savage could have walked it in a few minutes, but Crowther wanted to arrive in style. He wore evening clothes and sat in his carriage with Savage beside him while the driver expertly handled a pair of greys.

Shadows between lighted windows made for poor visibility. At least he'd agreed not to light the carriage lamps after Savage pointed out they made him an easy target.

This was a different Crowther, letting his hair down to try his luck at the turn of a wheel; without female company, but in the company of well-heeled gamblers.

The driveway they turned into was already filled with carriages; trees and shrubs made patches of shadow where a marksman could wait in ambush. The front door was wide open and light from within showed men in evening dress smoking cigars and holding glasses in the porch.

'Wait,' Savage said as the driver brought them to a halt, but Crowther was impatient to join his friends and stepped to the ground.

There came a sudden rush of men from the trees and a muttered, 'Do 'im!'

Savage glided into shadow as bodies hurled

themselves at Crowther; the banker went down, cursing. A gun exploded, a knife flashed. Someone screamed. The light from the doorway showed drinkers scattering while an angry voice shouted, 'Call the police!'

A horse, startled, reared up and its driver fell as the animal bolted. There was noise and confusion, but the target was obviously Crowther.

Savage recognized the accents of the ambushers. They were some of the same Australians who had attacked him with Clay.

He dived across Crowther as he struggled to get to his feet, knocking him flat again. 'Stay down,' he hissed. Covering Crowther's body with his own, he brought up his shotgun and squeezed one trigger.

The blast threw a man backwards, his flesh shredded, and Savage angled for another target.

'Bloody hell!' an Aussie muttered.

'Kill this interfering bastard,' Bruce snarled.

Savage turned to get a clear view of the gang leader, kicking another man in the face, and let Bruce have the second barrel. He drew his Bowie and struck out.

Some of the gang retreated in confusion, swearing, as whistles sounded and uniformed policemen arrived. Others made a last attempt to reach Crowther but were driven off.

Jerry Crowther picked himself up, unsteady and

breathing hard. He beat the dust from his clothes. A policeman looked at Bruce's body and then at Savage's shotgun as he reloaded.

Crowther had got his breath back. 'This man is my personal bodyguard, and doing what I pay him to do. So get after those Australian criminals and charge them with attempted murder.'

'Of course, JC.' The man touched his hat.

Crowther strode towards the gambling house, trailed by Savage. 'Somebody give me a drink.' He walked into the gaming room where, despite the shooting, men still watched the revolving wheel and calculated odds. He rubbed his hands in anticipation.

'Gentlemen, I'm feeling lucky tonight!'

When Monty came away from the gambling house, he was not pleased. That Savage should hire out to Crowther disturbed him: that he should kill Bruce alarmed him.

As he walked down the hill, he swung his cane vigorously; if one of Frisco's thugs should try anything at the moment, he'd get the heavy end across his face. He reached his office and found Frank Abbey waiting.

'What happened?' Abbey asked.

'Your private detective killed the leader of the Australian gang, defending Jerry Crowther. Why bother? I wish I knew what double game he's playing.'

Abbey kept quiet. He knew Savage's plan, knew this lawman wouldn't approve.

Monty scowled. 'There was a kind of balance before, one gang keeping the other in check. Now the New Dragon tong will have an edge and can take advantage of the situation. This could be bad news for honest citizens.'

He stroked his beard, considering options.

'The Aussie reaction to the Chinese trying to take control is likely to be violent, so there's going to be trouble.'

'How will that affect Barbara?'

'Who knows? I don't. Have you got that map Savage drew?'

Abbey pulled it from his pocket and spread it out on the office desk. They both studied it.

'I'm going to try to reach her,' Abbey declared, 'and to hell with Mr Wu.'

Monty had made up his mind. 'And I'll come along. We'd best move before the Aussies go hog-wild.'

Abbey felt better immediately. If a city detective investigated, surely even Mr Wu wouldn't lift a hand against them? And if they could reach Barbara, they could bring her out.

A police carriage carried them directly to

Chinatown, and Monty led the way along an alley to a herbalist's shop. Already extra police were patrolling the area, expecting trouble. Even though the night was dark, the shop was brightly lit and full of colour and exotic scents, with Cherry Blossom in attendance.

'Monty!' she exclaimed, apparently pleased to see him. 'And another friend. I am honoured. Will you take tea with me?'

'Not this time.' Monty was brusque. He jerked open the curtain at the back of the shop and pushed Abbey through and urged him up the stairs.

'Use the gun as a threat if you have to, but don't even think of using it. We'd be mobbed. Our best chance is to move fast.'

They went up and down stairs and along passages, following Savage's map, until a giant Chinese blocked their way.

'No trouble, Kong,' Monty warned.

'No trouble,' the big wrestler echoed, and took Abbey's shotgun from him and bent the barrel into a U-shape. He handed it back.

Monty showed his police badge and Kong said, 'We know who you are. Please hand me your gun.' Monty reluctantly obeyed. 'Mr Wu will grant you an audience if you will follow me.'

'He will, will he?'

They continued their journey, past closed doors and the suit of armour to the dragon curtain. Kong swept it aside. 'Enter.'

Wu sat smiling on his throne. 'Our police detective and—?'

'My name's Abbey and I've come for Miss Preston.'

'The man who deals in boots. You too are known, and will join her in a few minutes.'

Abbey said quickly. 'Monty doesn't know anything about Mr Savage's plan.'

'I should hope not.' Wu was at his most affable, seemingly amused by the situation. 'Sergeant – it is sergeant, isn't it?'

Monty nodded.

'I hear you are an honest man and that, no doubt, is why you have not been promoted further. You too will be my guest for a brief time. No harm will come to either of you.'

Wu brought a jade chessman from the sleeve of his kimono and tossed it from hand to hand as if he were a juggler.

'It seems the Australian barbarians are swarming like a disturbed nest of wasps, and I must ask you to be patient while I deal with them.'

He tossed the jade piece high and it vanished. Abbey blinked.

'As you know, sergeant, this tong is no threat to

other people of this city. We restrict our activities to our own race. I am asking you to wait patiently until Miss Preston can be safely released . . . Kong, escort our guests to the lady.

CHAPTER 13

TREMORS

Roo was celebrating. The minute he heard of Bruce's death, he bought the first round of drinks at the *Shamrock*. He called it a wake, of course, and the beer and whiskey flowed freely.

He was cautious, drinking only half a glass before refilling it. Other members of the gang were not so careful. He reckoned he was a natural to take over the gang and anyone who disagreed was going to regret it.

'We've got to get the bloke who done for Bruce,' one of the hoodlums kept mumbling.

'We will,' Roo promised, 'as soon as we've dealt with the slit-eyes. I didn't kill a warder, cross a desert to escape and travel halfway round the world to let a bunch of Chinks take over our rackets. So first we deal with the little yellow men, then we'll hunt down this Savage bloke.'

'Yeah,' another man agreed happily. 'Burn and loot, loot and burn, just like the old days. Here's to Chinatown!' He raised his glass in a drunken toast.

'Keep your noise down,' Roo hissed. 'We don't want everyone to know what's on.'

'That's right. Listen to Roo – he's an old hand at this game and knows what's what.'

They continued drinking and, behind the counter, Irish kept a vary eye on then and her sawn-off billiard cue close to hand. The *Shamrock* had been burnt down once before and she didn't intend to allow it to happen again.

Roo adjusted his bandage, mumbling, 'Christ, my head still hurts. Guess I'll get some air.'

He slammed down his empty glass on the table and went out into the night; stars twinkled over the ocean. One by one members of the gang followed.

Irish waited until the last of them had gone, then scribbled a note, sealed it with wax and gave it to an old man half asleep at a corner table.

'Take this to Monty, and there's a free drink when you come back.

Bob Leake felt sure his benefactor was Australian; the crude accent gave him away. He was also confident he could take care of this private bodyguard.

Leake had never lacked confidence in himself. It was just bad luck that his tongue had a life of its own, that his bragging caused more successful criminals to call him 'Leaky'. And because he couldn't be trusted to keep his mouth shut, Leaky remained a smalltime crook. A small man with big ideas, he was always on the verge of big things but never a part of them.

Always hard up, always looking for his big chance; and this could be it.

After their leader had been killed, naturally the Aussies would want revenge, so why this charade? A mask to hide his features, hoarse whispers in a shadowed doorway. Silly!

But there had been nothing silly about the used bank-notes pressed into his hand, with the promise of more to cone. Keeping quiet about his good fortune was almost more than Leaky could cope with; he longed to shout the good news from a rooftop. But that would have to wait till he'd collected his final payment.

And it would be final for JC – and Savage too if he got in the way.

Below ground, Lew Preston had been hearing strange noises for some time, but refused to let them worry him. He knew that all sorts of rumbling sounds were transmitted through the earth, and he knew what to listen for; the sound of rock shifting overhead, the creaking of timber under strain. These were nothing like that.

He was hot and sweaty at the work face, shifting rubble slowly and carefully to avoid alerting anyone above. The tunnelling had almost ended; now they had to go up, into the vault.

The rubble was placed carefully on one of the two wheeled platforms he'd had made specially and, equally carefully, dragged by rope to the shop's cellar and then removed by horse and cart.

So far the job had gone smoothly, his Chinese workers efficient. Now it was time to go outside, to organize the fireworks display that would cover the noise of their breakthrough. And to see Savage so he could deal with Crowther and Nolan.

And all the while he never forgot this was for Barbara, to get her away from Mr Wu's tong . . . he began to shake. Mostly he could control his fear but, every now and again, it rose like a tidal wave, swamping him. He had to get out in the open again.

He crawled after one of the platforms, to the cellar, pausing only long enough to swill water around inside his mouth to wash out the dust.

He came out to what sounded like a riot; shouting, guns going off, screaming and knives flashing. He saw men running with flaming torches and others battling with uniformed policemen. Whistles blew to summon reinforcements.

'Burn the yellow devils out!' a voice bawled, while other men looted shops.

Preston had never appreciated how near the bank was to Chinatown until he saw a crowd of Chinese armed with hatchets coming his way.

Their leader, a bald giant, addressed him by name. 'Get off the street, Mr Preston – get on with your work and leave the barbarians to us!'

It appeared that a gang of hoodlums was determined to attack Chinatown and the police were outnumbered. The Chinese were fighting for survival. A hatchet sliced and a man shrieked. The sky flushed red with dawn; soon it might be red with blood and fire.

Preston thought the giant was right; it was dangerous out here. He turned around, about to retreat into the shop when something struck him down from behind and he slumped to the ground.

Savage was late learning of the Aussies clash with police and Chinamen below the hill. Crowther's luck had held at the gaming table so it was two o'clock before he retired and Savage got a brief spell of sleep.

He had expected a late rising, but Crowther was up early, eager to make more money. After breakfast, the carriage was brought around to the front door. Jerry Crowther, always in a hurry, stepped outside. Savage pulled him back and pushed him down as a small man wearing a big hat and holding a revolver called out:

'This is the end for you, JC. You've been judged and found guilty. If there is a hell, I hope you're wearing asbestos skivvies.'

Savage felt a warning prickle at the back of his skull: *danger*. He ignored the small man: neighbours were already hurrying towards him and one called, 'What's the game, Leaky?'

Savage's gaze roved the area till it fixed on a clump of bushes and a slight movement as the early morning sun reflected off the barrel of a rifle. It was the hidden marksman who was the real danger.

He brought up his shotgun, finger curled around the first trigger: about to send a hail of shot, he recognized Albert Nolan and shifted his aim a fraction to miss the double-crossing banker. He didn't want Nolan out of the frame yet.

Crowther picked himself up as a couple of his neighbours grabbed hold of Leaky and disarmed him. He glared at his bodyguard. 'And what the hell were you doing?'

Savage gestured towards the bushes. 'The real killer was there. This man' – he indicated Leaky –

'was just a decoy.'

'Well, get afer him!'

'Too late. You can bet he had his escape route laid on.'

Crowther returned his gaze to Leaky. 'At least we've caught this one.' His tone was venomous. 'Now kill him!' He frowned as Savage shook his head.

'Let him go. I want him to talk – maybe it'll trick the real killer into thinking we know who he is.'

'One of those crims from Downunder,' Leaky said. 'You can rely on that.'

'It's likely enough.' A neighbour was eager to share the news. 'They raided Chinatown during the night, burning and looting—'

Now Crowther was keen to make sure his bank was still standing. They drove down in the carriage, viewing a scene of destruction.

'It could have been worse,' Crowther said. 'It has been in the past.'

Savage wondered if all the people of this city were mad, but only nodded. His job was to neutralize both Crowther and Nolan when Lew and his Chinese miners broke through from below into the bank's vault.

He kept looking, but saw no sign of either Preston or Monty. When they reached the bank, the front door was just being opened for public business, and Nolan showed little surprise at seeing his boss arrive early.

'No trouble, JC. We've weathered another storm.'

'I want to see for myself.'

'Of course.'

Savage noted that Nolan had not entirely escaped; a patch of paper stuck to his cheek disguised where a shotgun pellet had struck home.

'Cut myself shaving,' he explained easily, and winked at him.

He assumes he can buy my silence, Savage thought, and that suits me.

Nolan followed his boss, and Savage followed him, noting the hide-out gun under his coat. Even a brief inspection convinced Crowther there was nothing obviously wrong, and Nolan lit a cigar.

'Now I'll see the vault,' Crowther said.

Nolan was taken aback, and Savage tensed. But the manager blew a smoke ring and smiled. 'You can't imagine anyone could get that far, even if they did succeed in breaking in.'

Crowther repeated, 'Now I'll see the vault.'

Floating like rafts on a sea of molten lava, two of the gigantic slabs of rock making up the earth's crust grated one against the other, setting up shock waves that travelled through the planet.

Rock compressed here and expanded there: friction released heat. Stress deformed the hardest rock and strain began to build. Underground water lubricated before it turned to steam.

Like a snake ready to shed its skin, the earth flexed. Locally, one plate rode upwards while the other slid underneath. The planet's crust folded and rock shifted, slipped and fractured.

With the first tremors, rats deserted cellars, dogs went mad and birds left their trees. The planet vibrated like a harp string suddenly plucked and shudders shot through apparently solid foundations.

Lew Preston recovered quickly after being dragged under cover by one of the hatchetmen. 'You stay,' he was told. Another Chinese looked at his bloodied head and dismissed the injury. 'It is nothing, a bruise, the skin broken is all.'

Preston went into the cellar and crawled back along the tunnel, relieved to be where he knew what he was doing. His head ached and he felt dizzy, but it seemed he had suffered no serious damage. He would have to wait for the riot to stop.

He reached the end of the tunnel to supervise the first attack on the cement above when he felt the ground shift under his boots. A shower of dirt fell, blinding him. He knew instantly what was happening: an earthquake. Frisco was notorious for them, of course, but to be underground when one struck alarmed him.

'Everyone out,' he yelled. 'Down tools and get out now!' His translator was one of the first to bolt.

His fear vanished. He knew what he had to do – get his crew out, with himself last of all.

'This isn't the right moment, Frank,' Red Preston murmured, 'but I'll give your proposal serious consideration after we get out of here.'

Frank Abbey had once again proposed marriage, to Li Han's amusement. 'So romantic, you barbarians!' Perhaps the fact that they were both in chains suggested she couldn't run out on him this time.

Monty, testing his own chain, securely cemented into the cellar wall, considered Abbey the ultimate optimist. But the redhead was something else. Her missing finger still bothered her, and she kept the stump hidden from Abbey; he suspected she didn't have marriage on her mind at that moment.

Come to that he didn't take kindly to being chained up himself, and Mr Wu was going to learn it didn't pay to upset one of San Francisco's finest. It was damp and chilly in the cellar, although the elderly Chinese appeared to be at home down here.

A deep rumbling sound echoed far below, and the floor suddenly rippled as if it were a body of water. 'Quake,' Monty shouted in alarm, and tugged furiously at the chain holding him.

Nolan opened the door at the rear of the bank to show the vault. It appeared to be untouched and Savage, standing back, felt relief.

Crowther inspected the iron bars of the cage and its contents carefully while his manager, looking relaxed, enjoyed his cigar. Too relaxed, Savage thought and slowly brought up his shotgun.

Crowther said, 'Use your key, Albert – I'm going inside.'

As Nolan put his hand in his pocket, Crowther's face registered alarm. 'What's that?'

Savage had expected Chinese fireworks, but this was scary.

From below came the grating sound of rock snapping under pressure. All three stood transfixed; this was more than a tremor. Nolan moistened his lips and croaked, 'Earthquake!'

They were given no time to withdraw. The floor heaved upwards and then collapsed under them.

CHAPTER 14

THE DRAGON ROARS

From the window where she took her turn watching the entrance, Nell Merritt saw Savage and Crowther walk into the bank. For a while nothing happened and she grew bored.

'How about a coffee, Dave?'

Her husband was working on his book about the rail journey from the east. 'Give me a couple of minutes to finish this bit and I'll—'

There was a sudden shocking wrench and the road outside heaved up, tilted and slid away, leaving a wide crevasse. Nell watched a horse and cart disappear into it.

She gave a short shrill scream that startled Dave into looking around. The wall of their apartment

144

cracked and the window frame fell out. He jumped up to pull Nell back in time to see, across the street, the wall of Crowther's bank come tumbling down. Then a pall of dust obscured his view.

'Earthquake! Nell, hurry, we've got to get out of here.'

He pushed her towards the stairs, already creaking and splintering. 'Jump,' he shouted as they reached the bottom few steps.

Outside, panic had people running every which way, dodging falling chimneys, cannoning off each other. It was like walking into a nightmare. . . .

Cherry Blossom was one of the first to act. The local baker's shop had split in two and one half fallen into a pit, which had closed over. She borrowed the handcart the man used for deliveries and loaded her few possessions onto it. She helped herself to a handful of ginseng roots and set off.

Instead of making for the harbour as most did – in hope of escaping by boat – she trundled her cart uphill to the family home.

Her aunt ran the family as if she were an Empress and her husband a toy consort, but she wouldn't turn her away. Family was important, and her aunt would do almost anything for ginseng. So Cherry Blossom would wait it out, confident that not even an earthquake could unseat the family matriarch.

*

Mr Wu staggered as if from a blow. For once, he was taken by surprise. A wall drape dropped to the floor to reveal a leaning wall with a vertical crack.

He realized what was happening because he knew this city was prone to earthquakes, but this was the first one he'd experienced. He couldn't judge how serious it was, and felt uneasy.

Briefly, he considered his prisoners in the cellar, and dismissed them from his mind. They'd served their purpose. Li Nan was old; he shrugged – even the old had to die sometime.

It was the tunnel leading to the vault in Crowther's bank and a fortune that was important. Was the tunnel at risk? How close to success were his miners?

He paced like a caged animal, up and down, up and down. Not even a chess problem could calm his mind now.

A dusty gloom settled over the room and the strange silence was disturbed only by a creaking of old timbers. He signalled for tea, but no servant came.

He wrapped his kimono tighter about him and wondered: where was everybody? Where was Kong?

*

Roo has scared. Nothing in his experience had prepared him for this. He'd always relied on Bruce to do his thinking for him, and now what was left of his gang looked to him to save them.

His mind a blank, he could think of nothing to say until the road in front of them opened and the far side dropped away to reveal a frightening emptiness and a stomach-churning smell.

Then he said, 'Run like hell,' and turned around and set an example.

Kong wiped dust from his shaven head. The Aussies had run like rabbits when the road opened and the Earth Dragon roared. That was satisfying, but it seemed the Dragon was not yet ready to go back to sleep; it had not claimed enough sacrifices. Mouths still yawned wide to swallow many barbarians.

The old gods were not to be mocked as the white devils would learn.

The hatchetmen vanished as silently as they had appeared. Police tried to clear the streets in an attempt to save lives. Buildings slid gracelessly into a pile of bricks.

Kong returned to the empty shop as he saw tong miners coming out. He frowned. 'Why have you stopped work?'

The Chinese looked unhappy. 'White boss say to leave.'

Preston came outside, blinking. 'It's not safe down there till the quake's over. There are falls, and some props are giving way.'

'Safe? Mr Wu has given an order – to break into the vault. Clear the tunnel again, if necessary, but bring out the money. All of it.'

Preston started to protest. 'No, I can't allow—'

Kong felled him with one blow. 'Back to work,' he ordered.

The shop front collapsed. The road gaped like a hungry mouth and miners scattered.

Kong stepped back as the Earth Dragon roared again. He feared no man, but the gods were another natter: they demanded respect, He turned and hastened away to Wu's headquarters for fresh orders.

Ruby came out of Blumfield's, both hands filled with shopping, as the quake struck. The front of the store exploded, showering her with shards of glass. She dropped her shopping. She felt as if she wore being flayed, and screamed as blood ran down her face and her sight failed.

'Help me, someone help me – I can't see!'

Most people ignored her as they ran for their lives, but one hand reached out to grab her arm, pulling her into a narrow alley alongside the store. She stumbled, sobbing.

'My shopping! I must—'

Hands tore at her dress, forcing her onto her back in damp and smelly rubbish. She heard a young man's voice, trembling with excitement.

'I know you, even if you don't know me. I've been watching you, see, because I fancy you. You're JC's whore, and now it's my turn. No one's going to help you. . . .'

He sprawled on top of her, opening his pants. Glass dug into her back and she cried out, 'Wait, for God's sake! Let me—'

She heard a sound like a long roll on drums, growing louder, coming closer.

Then a bunch of terrified horses, broken free of their stabling, charged down the narrow alley, iron-shod hoofs pounding, stamping rapist and victim into unfeeling pulp.

Savage fell into darkness. He made himself relax, stifling panic. He recalled how he'd once been trapped in a gold mine in the mountains and got out, to quieten his nerves.

He hit soft dirt studded with pieces of stonework. The rumbling sound went on and falling bricks and chunks of cement were still coming down, burying him. He struggled to keep his head up and his arms free.

Someone moaned. Crowther? Nolan? Was there

anyone else down here? Dust threatened to choke him and he worked his coat up over his mouth and nostrils.

He heard a match strike and remembered that Nolan was a smoker. The brief flame revealed the manager's position and Savage kept still and quiet.

A voice spluttered, 'I can't move – help me, one of you.'

Through the dust, he glimpsed Crowther. The banker was pinned to the ground by part of the iron cage, which had collapsed and fallen across his legs.

Nolan laughed. 'It took an earthquake to get you where I want you, Jerry. Bruce failed, but I shan't.'

The flame died and Savage heard a gunshot. There was no further sound from Crowther, and rubble and dust continued to fall sporadically.

Nolan called softly, 'Are you there, Savage?'

He kept quiet, listening to Nolan trying to free the himself: the sounds pin-pointed the manager in the dark. He'd lost his grip on his shotgun in the fall so he drew his Bowie.

He waited in the darkness, sure he could outwit Nolan. Presently he heard the sounds of metal being pushed and pulled, ragged breathing. More debris fell and Nolan cursed.

He struck another match and Savage saw he was

150

trying to reach the money in the ruins of the metal cage; robbing his own bank. Still Savage waited, to allow Nolan to clear the way for him.

The match went out and, cautiously, Savage edged closer, pausing at the sound of yet another fall. This was mostly dust and he waited. His inclination was to dig his way out, but he didn't want to leave Nolen with a gun at his back.

He snaked forward, an inch at a time, his knife ready to strike.

'Goddamn,' Nolan suddenly muttered, spluttering dust and wrenching at the twisted iron rods. 'Move, damn you!' He sneezed.

Savage moved fast, leaping forward to push Nolan's face into the dirt. Holding him down with his weight, Savage felt with the tip of his knife for a gap between the ribs, slid the blade in and rammed it home. Nolan shuddered once and collapsed.

Savage waited till he was sure he was no longer breathing, then withdrew the knife and wiped it clean.

He waited, listening to small falls, then felt in his pocket for the matches he carried, wrapped in wax paper; more than once they'd proved their value in a tight corner.

He struck one and held up the flame to study the hole he'd dropped into: and realized it was the

151

tunnel Preston had been digging to reach the bank vault.

Climbing back up, with stuff still falling would be next to impossible; clearing Preston's tunnel offered an alternative escape route. But first he reached between the cage bars to take a packet of banknotes and stow them away in his pocket. Then he used his knife to start digging a way out.

With both Crowther and Nolan out of the running, he reckoned he could reach Chinatown and the cellar where Red was held prisoner. Maybe she was still alive, maybe not, but he had to try.

He soon realized it was not going to be easy. As he dug forward, inch by inch, the roof fell in behind him. He scraped away earth and broken rock, aware that the air was getting bad.

It was becoming harder to breathe and he felt his strength failing. He paused for a moment, and a trickle of dust continued to fall, filling the small space he occupied. It covered his head, forcing his shoulders down until he felt trapped.

Leaky was not discouraged by a mere earthquake. For him, it was an opportunity to take what others left behind in their blind panic. Where some people worried about their survival, Leaky knew he could do more than just survive. His confidence was never dented.

He still had most of that first payment from his benefactor; the Aussies had cleared off, so there was no chance of more there. But as his common-law wife, Clara, was fond of saying, 'One door closes, another opens'. She was still around somewhere, with a couple of kids and, like himself, a natural survivor.

He sniffed the air, smelling smoke. Further along the block he glimpsed the red glow of fire.

A hand took a firm grip on his arm. 'You! You'll take my orders now.'

The speaker was one of those pompous nobodies who take any opportunity to put on a uniform and give orders.

'We need to create a fire-break to stop the flames spreading. I have explosives on this wagon.'

It was more of a handcart and the man pushing it looked unhappy.

'Your luck's in,' Leaky said quickly. 'I know about explosives, so I'll take over for you.'

He grabbed the handles of the small barrow and briskly wheeled it away. Leaky had no doubt he could find a better use for this stuff: he dreamed of jewels for Clara, toys for the kids and the contents of a safe for himself.

CHAPTER 15

HUSBAND-IN-WAITING

Lew Preston picked himself up. He felt dazed, punch-drunk almost. In his early days as a mining engineer he'd met some scrappers, and again on the railroad, but Kong was in a class of one. He blinked at the ruin of a city, not quite taking it in; wrecked streets and the shells of buildings, dust and smoke and broken pipes leaking water; people running, crying and brawling. Barbara was some-where in this chaos and he didn't know where to look for her, except that she was someplace in Chinatown.

He felt close to despair when he heard scuffling

x

154

sounds from the empty shop behind him. Someone was trying to find a way out.

He stepped down into the cellar, seized a shovel and started to dig. Earth and debris fell steadily, refilling the tunnel as he tried to unblock it. The battle seemed endless.

He cast around outside until he found a length of pipe that had been broken off and carried it down to the cellar. He thrust it through the rubble filling the tunnel; at least some air might get through. He paused to listen and was rewarded by the sound of renewed digging; the pipe had reached whoever was trapped.

Now he used a pick to pull away the loose stuff from the entrance until a hand broke through, gripping a large Bowie knife, then a head with a dirty face gulping down air.

'Mr Savage!' Preston recovered enough to ask, 'Do you know where Barbara is?'

Savage practised breathing while he considered his answer. 'I know where she *was*.'

He set off towards Chinatown, followed by Preston. Here and there among the ruins a fire flickered, fanned by the wind, and clouds of smoke rose to a dusty sky. Flames leapt from one building to the next while firefighters stood by helplessly; the city's water pipes had been ruptured.

As the wind carried burning garbage to start

fresh fires, the blaze spread and the city burned. A scene from hell, Savage thought grimly; fire would finish what the earthquake had started.

'After we break her out,' he murmured, 'head for the waterfront. Get on a boat, any boat leaving harbour and heading for the other side of the bay.'

Chinatown was almost deserted; the last few families, their household goods piled onto hand barrows, were evacuating the area. There was a stink of smoke everywhere.

The blaze was still spreading, so they didn't have long to rescue the prisoner. Prisoners? Savage wondered what had happened to Abbey and Monty.

Looters were smashing their way into deserted shops and stores, and armed vigilantes shooting looters as they carried off stolen property.

Men used doors or wet sacks to protct themselves as they escaped the flames, and soldiers struggled to create a fire-break. Heat came in waves, driving everyone to find cover.

Just across the way from the herbalist's a sheet of flame roared out from a house as a window collapsed, scattering a pack of scavenging dogs.

'Come on, in here,' Savage said, plunging into the shop.

Cherry Blossom had gone and he made for the stairs, taking them two at a time. The smell of smoke reached even here, pungent and choking. He had to go up to find his way down to the cellar; it was the only route he knew and there wasn't anybody left to ask.

Preston followed blindly, up, down, past silent rooms with doors standing wide; the inhabitants had obviously fled. Walls leaned and floors gaped – Savage jumped these. The heated air was stifling.

He reached the dragon curtain and ripped it aside; the throne room was empty.

He went through the doorway behind the throne and started down. After a while he sensed it wasn't Preston following behind and glanced back and up: *Kong*.

The large Chinese said, 'Mr Wu is not pleased. You have failed to produce money from the vault, so—' He made a throat-cutting gesture.

Savage stood motionless, looking up, facing Kong. 'It's a sure thing he couldn't do it himself. Any more than I could take you in a fair fight – but this isn't going to be fair.'

'Mr Wu is preparing to leave this city—'

'Wise of him. I'll just collect Miss Preston and leave too.'

Savage turned and started down the stairs again, and Kong came after him. He descended quickly so the big Chinaman worked up some momentum.

Then he sat down. Hurrying, Kong tripped and

stumbled. Savage seized him in a wrestling grip and fell forward, pulling Kong over his head and releasing him.

The giant plunged headlong down the flight of bare wooden stairs, his skull crashing on each tread. He landed at the bottom, hardly conscious.

Savage gave him no time to recover. He jumped, landing with both feet on his chest and forcing the air from his lungs.

He grabbed Kong by the ears and wrenched his head around in one quick movement. He heard the neck snap.

Savage stood up, listening. He called, 'Mr Preston?' There was no answer and he continued down to the cellar.

Monty had one foot braced against the wall and the slack of his chain in both hands and was pulling with every bit of strength he possessed. It didn't seem to make any difference and he was feeling desperate.

Red Preston copied him and her bit of wall collapsed. She staggered free and almost fell, quick-stepping to keep her balance. 'I knew that dancing class would come in useful one day,' she muttered.

She weighed the length of chain attached to her wrist considering it as a weapon. 'Don't worry, old man,' she told Li Han. 'I won't take it out on you.'

Frank Abbey, a bit slow to catch on, began to tug on his chain. She gave him a sweet smile. 'Don't let it worry you, Frank; just try to get used to it being me who does any necessary rescuing.'

The door was unbarred from the outside and Savage walked in.

'Mr Savage, will you look after Frank for me? I'll be back for him after I've settled with Mr Wu.'

As he set about freeing Monty and Frank Abbey, she went past him at a brisk trot, through the doorway and climbed over Kong's body, sparing a moment to wonder how Savage had done it. She'd have to ask him later to add to her own repertoire of dirty tricks.

She went up the stairs till she reached a huge suit of armour, and paused, admiring. A phrase came to mind: 'they were giants in those days'.

She could smell smoke, and one wall was hot to touch. Wu's inner room must be close, she thought when a voice hissed 'The barbarian woman!'

She turned to see Wu standing only a few yards away, dressed for travelling and holding a small suitcase.

'You have caused trouble,' he continued. 'Too many things have gone wrong since you came here. Now I must return to my own land but, before I go, this wrong-doing must end.'

He set down his suitcase and straightened to his full height, like a bird of prey about to strike. He brought a revolver from beneath his coat and aimed it at her, holding it steadily in two hands and prepared to take his time over the execution.

Red Preston was not impressed: she remembered her old school's motto: 'Anything a man can do, we can do better'. And Wu was only a man dressed up.

She didn't hesitate, but turned to the suit of armour and seized hold of the great sword with both hands. It was heavy and took all her strength to raise it . . . the floor shook with yet another tremor and the weight of the iron blade fell across Wu's shoulders.

A look of surprise crossed his face and his finger jerked the trigger of his revolver. Not even Red could have said where the bullet went.

Wu's head hit the floor and rolled down the stairs to end up next to Kong.

She watched with satisfaction. 'A head for a finger,' she murmured, and followed it down to claim her husband-in-waiting.

Frank Abbey had followed her doggedly and risked his life. He deserved his reward, and Dad could seek finance from her new father-in-law.

And Savage? Red smiled. There would be time before her marriage to bid him a proper goodbye!

RJ
PR.